DOCTOR WHO
THE
CHRISTMAS INVASION

Based on the BBC television adventure *The Christmas Invasion* by Russell T Davies

JENNY T. COLGAN

BBC
BOOKS

3 5 7 9 10 8 6 4

BBC Books, an imprint of Ebury Publishing
20 Vauxhall Bridge Road,
London SW1V 2SA

BBC Books is part of the Penguin Random House group of companies whose
addresses can be found at global.penguinrandomhouse.com

Penguin
Random House
UK

Novelisation copyright © Jenny T. Colgan 2018
Original script copyright © Russell T Davies 2005

Jenny T. Colgan has asserted her right to be identified as the author of this
Work in accordance with the Copyright, Designs and Patents Act 1988

Doctor Who is a BBC Wales production for BBC One.
Executive producers: Steven Moffat and Brian Minchin

First published by BBC Books in 2018

www.penguin.co.uk

A CIP catalogue record for this book is available from the British Library

ISBN 9781785943287

Editorial Director: Albert DePetrillo
Project Editor: Steve Cole
Cover design: Two Associates
Cover illustration: Anthony Dry
Production: Phil Spencer

Typeset in 11.4/14.6 pt Adobe Caslon Pro
by Integra Software Services Pvt. Ltd, Pondicherry

Printed and bound in Great Britain by Clays Ltd, St Ives PLC

Penguin Random House is committed to a sustainable future for our
business, our readers and our planet. This book is made from
Forest Stewardship Council® certified paper.

MIX
Paper from
responsible sources
FSC
www.fsc.org   FSC® C018179

Contents

Prologue

There is a moment: a terrible moment, when you wake up, and you suddenly realise, to your panic, that you've missed something.

Perhaps you've missed the train to your first day at a new job, or the school bus, and there's an important exam.

Perhaps you wake up and for a moment think that someone you knew is with you; someone you loved still loves you back, and then your stomach drops like an express elevator, as you remember once again that they are gone; or that they are dead.

Maybe you dreamt that you lost something—that it has tumbled into the water, out of reach, further and further and you cannot grab hold of it, no matter how you try, you can only watch it go—but then you wake up and it was a dream all along and you feel utter, earthshattering relief.

But sometimes the dream is golden and full of every piece of knowledge about the universe and ultimate

1

power and glorious resurrection—and then you wake up and realise that all of that has crumbled into dust.

And the reality is, somebody—something—in the shape of a man has eaten your best friend, and it's standing right in front of you and it's talking about Barcelona, of all things, and it absolutely will not shut up and you have no idea what to do.

Rose Tyler crouched by the pillars of the TARDIS console room, the afterglow of the extraordinary golden light still visible on the inside of her eyelids; burned on her retinas—and felt more frightened and alone than she'd ever felt in her life.

1

Joy to the World

If you have ever been to an industrial park—which is a terrible misnomer, because they are literally the opposite of parks; they are factory farms for people—you will have seen a building like this. Low rise. Cheap brown bricks. Rows of identical windows with PVC frames because nobody cared enough, at any stage of its construction, to try to make it attractive, or interesting, or stand out in any way.

Usually these buildings—which do not have names, but numbers (this was 42)—end up this way because of laziness, or cost-cutting on the part of the kind of people who make business parks for a living; or people who are so devoid of imagination they think your environment does not matter to you.

In the case of Unit 42, Fanshield Industrial Park, though, this was not simply a product of end-stage capitalism. This was the entire point. If you had driven past it, you possibly wouldn't even have noticed it; a building so bland it slipped off the eye.

3

If you had, you might have thought, 'Whoa. Imagine having to spend your entire life in there.' In the highly unlikely event that you'd looked closer, you might have wondered why there was all that barbed wire; or why the security guards and janitors reception staff all looked like square-headed ex-marines—which they were.

Inside Industrial Unit 42, though, the atmosphere was actually incredibly exciting.

Because this low building off the ring road of Reading was in fact the centre of Britain's rocket-building programme, which recently—since Harriet Jones had been elected Prime Minister—had received a boost to its funding and undertaken a mission that had drawn envious stares from scientists and astronomers around the world.

Unit 42 was building *Guinevere*.

Guinevere was going to be the first drone ever to land on Mars. The first-ever footage from the red planet—from the actual solid dusty earth of the red planet—was soon to arrive; and it was going to be British engineering and a team of mostly British and European scientists that had made it happen. Behind the long rows of blacked-out windows, the mood was actually near-hysterical.

Meanwhile, the champagne delivery company had got lost. It had never had cause to deliver to the Fanshield Industrial Park before.

Inside the low brown building, Matthew Nicolson, senior programmer on UK Rocket Project 9.2, codename: Guinevere, pushed back from his low console, rocked in his chair a little to shift his position, wiped down his glasses and smiled to himself.

Next to him was Duerte Rodriguez, who was wearing shorts and sandals despite the fact that it was Christmas Eve. (Wearing shorts was Duerte's thing. Matthew had pointed out to him that if he wanted to become more attractive to women he should develop his personality rather than just his trousers. Duerte had immediately pointed out a) that Matthew already had a 'thing', namely his wheelchair, so he could shut up and also b) at least he, Duerte, could put on his own shorts. Matthew had tolerated this as he had a girlfriend and Duerte did not, and besides their friendship was practically predicated on Duerte making ridiculously offensive remarks about his chair, which was a relief when most people tried to tiptoe round it, literally and figuratively. They were good friends.)

'Why are you smiling?' said Duerte suspiciously.

Matthew pushed himself even further back from the console and made a 'ta-dah!' sign.

Duerte clocked it immediately. 'No way.'

'I would say do the math,' said Matthew. 'But I've seen you do math.'

'*Maths*,' said Duerte, shaking his head. But he scooted over his chair and peered more closely at the lines of code filling Matthew's screen. Then he whistled through his teeth. It looked like … it couldn't be. But it *looked* like *Guinevere One* was in position. It looked like they had the coordinates, the weather, the thruster fuel and the landing spot all lined up.

It looked as if *Guinevere One* was ready to land.

'Is she going down?'

'Locked and loaded,' said Matthew smugly. 'And all in time for Christmas.'

Luanne the press officer came charging past as usual. To Matthew and Duerte she seemed to be breezing constantly between appointments, despite the fact that, as the press officer for a top-secret government rocket facility, her job could surely only consist of her saying, 'Hello? No, we're not a top-secret government rocket facility' every time the phone rang. But she was mostly a good sort, Luanne. Well, when she wasn't bugging them about cleaning up the communal kitchen and begging Duerte to at least wear shoes so she didn't have to look at his disgusting horny toes all the time.

She swerved to a halt. Not much got past Luanne (which, as *she* would have told you, was her *actual* job).

'What was that blokey slang about? Does "locked and loaded" mean something good or something bad?'

'Rad and awesome,' said Matthew.

Looking at him now, Luanne knew exactly what he meant. They'd been waiting for this. This would be the time for her skills to truly come to the fore;

to announce to the world what they'd achieved. Excitement bubbled up.

'You're early,' she said, delightedly.

'I know,' said Matthew.

'He's going to be insufferable,' chimed in Duerte, 'for hours. Enough with the smugness, Nicolson, before I jam your spokes.'

'Try it and I will ram your shins, my friend.'

A huge smile stretched over Luanne's features. 'Can I make the call? Let me. Come on, it'll be fun, trying to get a smile out of Llewellyn. I don't think he's slept since Hallowe'en.'

Llewellyn was their young, grave boss; slender, bearded and with a clipped manner that seemed at odds with his gentle Valleys accent. They liked him and they respected him; he wasn't the sort you messed about.

'Shall we let her?' Matthew mused aloud.

Duerte shrugged. 'Girl's stealing all the credit as usual.'

Luanne stuck her tongue out at him, leaned over Matthew's shoulder and tapped a few buttons, calling up the live feed. Sure enough, there was the beautiful space probe, *Guinevere One*, hovering above Mars, her external cameras reflecting the light behind her. And Matthew was showing her, with total confidence, that the landing coordinates were set and ready to go. They all looked at it for a moment, smiling.

'She is so beautiful,' said Luanne.

'Still sad you didn't leave to work for John Lumic, Nicolson?' teased Duerte.

Matthew rolled his eyes. 'Two Ironsides together? No thanks. Though the money here is still shocking, by the way.'

Luanne pulled out her phone. More and more of the staff were coming over to congratulate them, realising what must have happened. It sounded like someone was popping a bottle of something fizzy in the adjoining communal area. Llewellyn came walking swiftly down the long dark corridor, the throng of other staff opening a way clear for him.

'We've done it!' said Luanne joyously.

'Uhm?' said Matthew.

Luanne rolled her eyes. '*The team* has done it,' she said, more slowly. Honestly, they thought she contributed nothing (they did think this).

Llewellyn checked the data very carefully and methodically, the way he did everything, as the others grew antsy with anticipation behind him. Finally he straightened up and gave as close to a smile as he could manage.

'Okay to go,' he said, quietly.

Luanne burst forward. 'I'll put it on speaker. You can all listen in whilst I talk… to the Prime Minister's office.' There were some whoops. 'Duerte, check the weather reports. Let's see if they fancy a bunch of Mars pictures… for Christmas Day!'

Someone cheered.

'Shh! Shh!' said Luanne. She dialled the number, then put it on speaker. It was answered promptly.

'Good morning, Downing Street,' came the officious voice. 'How can I help you?'

'Harriet Jones's office please... It's Guinevere.'

Only one word was ever needed from the industrial unit at 42 Fanshield Park.

'Putting you straight through.'

2

What Child is This?

'I don't want to go to Barcelona,' Rose said again, her voice sounding small and frightened in the huge console room. 'Please stop talking about Barcelona. I … I just want to go home.'

The TARDIS lurched once more; the wild-eyed figure staring at the controls as if it had never seen them before.

She glanced up.

'That's Earth. I live on Earth. In London.'

The figure swayed until she thought it was going to fall. Then it caught her eye.

'I know where you live, Rose.'

And she backed even further against the reassuring root of the console room strut, clinging on to it for comfort. This is what happens, she told herself, when you take wonders for granted. She hadn't even noticed when something had come and taken over the Doctor. Her Doctor.

They had flown so high, burned so brightly—and now they were crashing back to Earth, faster and faster; her and this…

This *what*?

She could not even look at what the Doctor had become. This… alien, who had treated her like someone he knew utterly and unquenchably. His partner. Hand in hand, until she had learned to trust that hand, until she had felt it naturally by her side as if it were a part of her. As if they were, almost, the same person.

Except, of course, he wasn't a person and she didn't know him at all. He had told her, but she hadn't understood and she hadn't wanted to understand. She'd wanted to believe they were the same; had wanted so much for that hand in hers to be forever.

And now he was dead, eaten by this thing that still dared to wear his clothes.

Rose hid behind the carved, tree-like pillar in the console room, which was stupid, as she could still be seen quite clearly. She glanced around. There wasn't much in the TARDIS you could use as a weapon. She stole a glance round. What was it doing? It was moving its mouth up and down. Her heart pounded faster. What had it done to him? A shapeshifter? She'd met all sorts…

It was wittering on. She stared at it, horrified and curious.

'I'm … Tuesday … October 500 … on the way to Barcelona …'

The thing in the Doctor's clothes wasn't making any sense. Was it regurgitating his brainwaves? She wanted to scream, tear into the thing, for what it had done, but she didn't dare approach it.

It straightened up and grinned at her in the most disarming way.

'Now then,' it said. 'What do I look like?'

Rose wondered if she could bring it down by the legs. Why wasn't the TARDIS doing something, like opening an airlock or something? She concentrated on thinking this as hard as she could so that the TARDIS might pick up on the idea, but nothing happened.

The thing held up its hand as if it had been expecting her to respond.

'No, no, no, nonononononononono. No. Don't tell me…'

It started shaking its hands and body up and down.

'Let's see… two legs, two arms, two hands… slight weakness in the dorsal tubercle…'

Its hands flew to its head.

'Hair! Oh, I'm not bald!'

Rose blinked. What on earth was it doing? She shifted forward an inch.

It carried on running its hands through its hair, a look of total surprise on its face.

'*Oh! Big* hair! … Sideburns!'

Now the creature sounded delighted.

'I've got sideburns! Or really bad skin. Little bit thinner.'

It slapped itself on the stomach.

'That's weird. Give me time, I'll get used to it.'

The face lit up suddenly, overjoyed.

'I have got a mole! I can feel it!'

It started wriggling about, gyrating its shoulders.

'Between my shoulder blades! There's a mole! That's all right. Love the mole.'

It grinned at her. Rose blinked. This was… Well. It couldn't be a person. But somehow after this weird review, it seemed less threatening.

It moved closer, its hair now a mess, and she shrank back instinctively.

'Go on then. Tell me. What do you think?'

Well, that was a question. She didn't know *what* she thought. Rose swallowed before she spoke and when her voice came out, it wasn't at all the strong commanding tones she had hoped for. Instead, she sounded timid, fearful, longing for something she couldn't put her finger on, something so impossible…

'I'm going to change.'

He had said that. He had said that, just before… but no. It couldn't. It couldn't be.

'Time Lords have this little trick.'

She looked at the figure in front of her again, which was still rumpling up its own face.

It couldn't be. Rose closed her eyes. What was happening? Then she opened them again, and took a deep breath. 'Who are you?'

The shape looked surprised, and not a little wounded. 'I'm the Doctor!'

Rose moved closer. 'No. Where *is* the Doctor? What have you done with him?'

She wished again she had a weapon, even if he—the real Doctor—would have been totally against that.

This person looked confused.

'But… you saw me. I changed… right in front of you.' He glanced over his shoulder to the spot by the console where she'd seen the light—that boiling exploding golden light shooting out from the Doctor.

Rose shook her head. 'I saw the Doctor sort of explode, and then you replaced him like… a… a teleport or a transmat or a body swap or something.' She stepped closer towards him, her anger rising, and pushed him full in the chest. 'You're not fooling me.'

The creature wobbled back on its heels as if it couldn't believe what it was hearing.

'I've seen all sorts of things. Nanogenes… Gelth… Slitheen… Oh my God, are you a Slitheen?'

The figure raised its eyebrows. 'I'm not a Slitheen.'

Rose shouted, all her fear and frustration coming out. 'SEND HIM BACK! I'M WARNING YOU! SEND THE DOCTOR BACK RIGHT NOW!'

'Rose, it's me. Honestly. It's me.'

Rose couldn't catch her breath. Her brain couldn't take in what he was saying.

'I was dying,' it said. 'To save my own life I changed my body. Every single cell, but… it's still me.'

'Time Lords have this little trick. It's a sort of a way of cheating death. Except it means I'm going to change.'

She'd heard it for herself, still couldn't believe her own eyes.

'You can't be.'

Time Lords have this little trick. It ran through her head, over and over. *This little trick.* Like it was only a bit of conjuring, a bit of fun. Just a prank to be played on primitive apes like her.

Now the figure moved towards her, closer, and looked her straight in the eye, his voice low. 'If I'm not him, how could I remember this? Very first word I ever said to you. Trapped in that cellar, surrounded by shop window dummies—oh!'

He seemed, suddenly, overwhelmed at the recollection, and Rose suddenly found herself back there too with him, for the very first time. Before everything in her world—in the entire universe—had changed. The very first moment.

'Such a long time ago,' he said. 'I took your hand.'

Rose flinched. Suddenly a hand—a different hand?—was in hers, as naturally as if it had always been there. She looked at it. He carried on talking, gentler now, as if trying to calm a frightened animal.

16

'I said one word… just one word, I said: "Run".'

But it didn't sound the same when he said it and his hand did not feel the same. Then he said it again, very, very quietly, and squeezed her hand… and suddenly, there it was, like a tolling bell. She felt it. Somehow, deep down, she knew. She couldn't prove it but—she had faith. She trusted him. She knew.

'I'm not going to see you again. Not like this. Not with this daft old face.'

Tears started to roll down her cheeks.

'Doctor,' she said, and her voice was a whisper.

The Doctor's voice was still gentle.

'Hello,' he said.

Then he dropped her hand, and Rose nearly tripped over backwards, a million questions burning through her brain. Was he the same man? How? Did he know everything? Did he feel the same way? Would he act the same way? Could he dance now?

The Doctor—this Doctor—had bounced back round the console.

'And we never stopped, did we? All across the universe. Running, running, running…'

He started messing about with the console, flicking switches without even glancing at them now; and the TARDIS was letting him, completely unconcerned.

'One time we had to hop. Do you remember? Hopping for our lives?'

He started hopping. Rose did not remember and stared at him. He slowed down.

'Yeah? All that hopping? Remember hopping for your life? Yeah? Hop? With the... no?'

Rose blinked.

'Can you change back?'

'Do you want me to?'

'Yeah.'

'Oh.'

'Can you?'

'No.'

The Doctor stared at his shoes. 'Do you want to leave?'

'Do you want me to leave?' Rose shot back straightaway.

'*No!* But... it's your choice. If you want to go home...'

Rose looked at him, her eyes sad.

'Cancel Barcelona,' he said suddenly. 'Change to... London. The Powell Estate. Ah, let's say... the 24th of December. Consider it a Christmas present.'

Rose moved towards him again, then hesitated, desperately confused as the Doctor hit the buttons.

'There.' The Doctor stood back and folded his arms, looking hurt as the TARDIS lurched to a sudden halt.

'I'm going home?' said Rose, feeling wounded.

'Up to you. Back to your mum. It's all waiting. Fish and chips, sausage and mash, beans on toast... No. No, it's Christmas. Turkey! Although… having met your mother… nut loaf would be more appropriate.'

Rose let out a short burst of surprised laughter.

'Was that a smile?'

'No.'

'That *was* a smile.'

'No it wasn't.'

'You smiled.'

'No I didn't!'

'Oh come on, all I did was change, I didn't—'

Out of the blue, his entire body took a sudden lurch, and his face changed. Rose's first thought was that he was about to be sick. She moved forward.

'What?'

'I said, I didn't—'

This time he collapsed over the console. Rose was really worried now and inched her way towards him.

'Uh-oh.'

The last thing Rose wanted to hear was 'uh-oh'. Uh-oh what? 'Uh-oh, I've finished eating the Doctor so it's time to start on you?' 'Uh-oh, I'm about to die for real this time and the TARDIS doors are going to lock forever?'

'Are you all right?'

She watched in awe as from out of the Doctor's mouth came a long line of the golden miasma; Rose knew, could *feel*, it was the same time vortex energy that she'd had inside her, just for a few moments—and it had nearly destroyed her. If the Doctor, *her* Doctor, hadn't drawn it out of her…

He—her Doctor. He had sent her away from Satellite Five, as he prepared to sacrifice himself to save the universe. The entire universe. And she hadn't been having any of it. She had opened the heart of the TARDIS. The oddest thing; she had absolutely no memory as to what had happened after that; only that when she had come back to herself the Daleks had gone. Jack was alive, thank God—and her head was splitting, a pain so immense and overwhelming she felt it would destroy her.

Then the Doctor had taken her pain away: all of it.

How, she thought, jolted back to a place she could barely remember—how could you be full of that; have that inside you; the void of the endless; the heart of everything that could ever be. How could you live like that and not turn completely mad…?

Oh my God, thought Rose. That was it. He'd turned completely mad.

'It's all right.' The man's voice sounded pained. 'The change is going a bit wrong, is all.' Now the pain was written all over his face, and he slumped down onto his knees.

Rose made a decision. She would have to trust him because otherwise she couldn't help him, and if she couldn't help him, there was no help for anything.

20

'Look… maybe we should go back. Let's go and find Captain Jack, he'd know what to do.'

The Doctor shook his head, grasping up to hold on to the console from the floor. 'Gah, he's busy! He's got plenty to do rebuilding the Earth.' He glanced up suddenly as his hand felt something, and his eye lit upon a large red lever. 'I haven't used this one in years.'

He flicked it, and the TARDIS suddenly jerked to the side violently, and they both nearly tumbled to the floor.

'What're you doing?' said Rose, panic gripping her.

'Putting on a bit of speed! That's it!'

Rose grabbed the console desperately.

'My beautiful ship! Come on, faster! Thassa girl!' His face was absolutely manic and terror gripped Rose. '*Faster!* Want to break the time limit?'

'STOP IT!' Rose couldn't take any more.

'Ah, don't be so dull… let's have a bit of fun! Let's rip through the time vortex!'

Rose didn't like this—this new version of the Doctor, this new *thing*. She glared at him. Then he caught her eye and gazed back at her and she felt it again; that odd, odd glimmer of recognition she had felt when he'd taken her hand.

His voice dropped.

'The regeneration's going wrong. I can't stop myself.' His face was a mask of pain as he jerked and twitched. 'Ah, my head.' Then he jumped back up again, the crazy look back on his face. 'Faster! Let's open those engines!'

Alarm bells were ringing, and not, Rose thought, just in the TARDIS.

'What's that?'

'We're gonna crash-land!' yelled the Doctor, his grin too wide for his face.

Rose shouted at him. 'Well, then do something!'

He was hysterical now.

'Too late! Out of control! Oh, I love it! Hot Dog!'

'YOU'RE GOING TO KILL US!'

'Hold on tight… Here we go…'

Rose was so frightened, so scared. Whoever this madman was, he was still grinning maniacally.

'CHRISTMAS EVE!'

3

Do You Hear What I Hear?

Jackie Tyler was listening to Christmas songs and decorating the old tree and telling herself that things could be worse.

She told herself that a lot, these days.

Things could definitely be worse. Debbie Pringle's daughter had got herself knocked up with triplets and all four of them were currently camping out in her front room.

'Must be nice, having babies about the place again,' she'd said to Debbie when they'd run into each other in the Costco, and Debbie, whose trolley was piled high with six boxes of nappies, eight tins of powdered milk and a bottle of unbranded vodka, had grabbed her wide-eyed and said, 'Take one! Take any one! I don't care which, they all look the same!' then shrieked when her phone rang and dashed off, trailing baby powder and a faint whiff of something else less pleasant in her wake.

And she could invite Howard round. Yeah. That'd be nice. Get some fruit in. Did they need a whole turkey?

Probably not. Maybe get one of those crowns. Wouldn't take up the whole oven, so that was nice.

Of course, she had a present for Rose. Of course she did. She'd keep it with the birthday present she'd popped back in the cupboard. Just in case she stopped by. And that top that she'd seen down the market; bright yellow, Rose would hate it. But it would light up her face. She looked good with a bit of colour.

Should she invite Mickey? It wasn't right, him being all alone like that at Christmas. On the other hand, whenever she saw Mickey, they tried and tried to avoid the subject and they'd manage for a bit, and then there'd be a pause in the conversation and then somebody— okay, her—would have a brandy and Coke too many and then it would all come out, the endless agony of missing someone so badly it felt like a hook caught in your side, all the time, snagging on everything you saw every day. No, seeing Mickey wouldn't help, especially not when he hit the brandy and Coke too.

Andy Williams started crooning 'It's the Most Wonderful Time of the Year'. Jackie considered throwing the CD player out of the window.

The good thing about me, thought Mickey, is that I'm good at compartmentalising.

In his weaker moments he thought it was just because he'd had so much practice; he'd managed with his gran, no bother, so he'd do it with Rose too, off getting up to God knows what with some stupid man in a stupid black leather jacket. As if he could compete with a stupid magic flying box. Stupid …

No. See, he reminded himself, grabbing a wrench with unnecessary force. Compartmentalising. That was what he was good at. Head down. Get on with the job—it wasn't bad at Alfie's garage, not at all, the lads were great, and they were going to have a drinks night out that would be a right laugh. Because he was good at compartmentalising so he was going to go out and have a night out and a curry and a…

'Merry Xmas Everybody' was screaming from the old radio in the garage. Work, Mickey knew, was the best way of getting over things. Everything. Just throw yourself into it. Never think about 'out there'. If you could talk about the match on Saturday, and fix a car…

If a car has something broken, you fix it, thought Mickey. You don't go all over space, you don't mess about in time. You replace the parts and then it works again and it's cause and effect and you don't need to even think about any of that other…

Oh God, what if she doesn't come home again?

That's exactly the kind of thing I'm not going to be thinking about, he told himself firmly.

He'd lost people before. The thought didn't cheer Mickey up any more than Slade blaring from the far-too-loud radio.

Thanks to Slade, it was Jackie who heard it first. The only sound she'd been waiting to hear. All this time, since she'd let her little girl go, again and again and again. She pretended it was fine; she pretended she was all right with her precious Rose—all she had in the world—vanishing with that dreadful man.

But there was still only one noise Jackie Tyler wanted to hear, and it was the signal that Rose was coming home. And she could hear it now. A grinding of phantom gears.

'Rose!'

Back in the garage, the Christmas music was still blaring. Mickey blinked. He was sure he could hear something, definitely sure. Something that sounded a little like… a strange, loud, wheezing noise.

'Hey, turn that down. Turn it off, Stevo. Turn that off! John, shut up!'

Sure enough, there it was. Clear as a bell.

Rose. She was back!

Mickey dropped his tools.

Mickey and Jackie almost collided down on the courtyard of the estate. A freezing wind blew through the concrete passageways; rattling the bin lids; sending crisp packets dancing around the flagstones.

'Mickey!'

Mickey was tearing towards her. 'Jackie, it's the TARDIS!'

'I know, I know, I heard it. She's alive, Mickey! I said so, didn't I? She's alive!'

'Just shut up a minute!' said Mickey, desperate to hear where the sound was coming from. He turned round and flinched as, suddenly, the TARDIS simply appeared from nowhere, bouncing through mid-air. It crashed into one of the estate blocks; rebounded, narrowly missing a Royal Mail van, and finally came to rest against a pile of dustbins.

Jackie and Mickey watched, terrified. The door opened slowly. And out came... a figure, dressed in a leather jacket about four sizes too large for him. They'd never seen him before.

'Here we are then. London. Earth. The Solar System. We did it. Jackie! Mickey! Blimey! No, no, no, no, hold on. Wait there. I've got something to say. There was something I had to tell you, something important. What was it? No, hold on, hold on. Hold on, shush, shush, shush, shush, shush. Oh, I know! Merry Christmas!'

Then the strange figure collapsed in a heap.

Rose emerged. Jackie gasped, but her daughter's attention was immediately on the splayed figure in front of the TARDIS.

'What happened? Is he all right?'

Mickey moved over. 'I don't know, he just keeled over. But who is he? Where's the Doctor?'

Rose quickly computed that she couldn't go through with trying to explain it. She didn't know how, and she didn't know if she believed it herself. Maybe if she pretended to be fine with it, they would be too.

'That's him, right in front of you,' she said, quickly. 'That's the Doctor.'

Jackie's relief and delight at seeing her daughter turned to exasperation as it quickly became clear that once again Rose was totally fixated on yet another weird stranger.

'What do you mean, that's the Doctor? Doctor Who?'

4

Lonely This Christmas

In the end, they'd dressed the strange thin man in pyjamas Jackie had produced from somewhere, and put him to bed. Nobody seemed to know quite what to do. Then Jackie briefly vanished and returned brandishing a stethoscope triumphantly.

'Here we go,' she announced. 'Tina the cleaner's got this lodger, a medical student, and she was fast asleep, so I just took it. Though I still say we should take him to hospital.'

Rose shook her head 'We can't. They'd lock him up. They'd dissect him. One bottle of his blood could change the future of the human race. No! Shush!'

Carefully, she inched up the bed, closer to him. It seemed just so strange; this odd person, who had once been the Doctor. She approached him carefully. He smelled the same, that was funny; that odd combination of chalk dust, boiled sweets, lime and diesel.

She carefully placed the stethoscope down, first on one side, then the other. The soft thump in her ears stayed steady. There he was. It was the Doctor, absolutely.

She thought this ought to make her feel better. Oddly, it didn't. It was a Time Lord, maybe. But it wasn't her Time Lord.

'Both working,' she announced.

'What do you mean, both?' said Jackie, who had her arms folded.

'Well, he's got two hearts,' explained Rose.

'Oh, don't be stupid,' said Jackie.

'He has.'

'Anything else he's got two of?'

'Leave him alone!!'

With one backwards glance, Rose led Jackie out of the room, leaving him to sleep. As they left, a further stream of TARDIS energy, golden in the atmosphere, left his body, unobserved; spun off into the universe; setting alarms; drawing attention.

Rose realised, suddenly, that she was starving. Food would help. She rifled in the fridge. She saw the little turkey crown, but didn't want to think about that right now. Instead she pulled out a mini pork pie, as Jackie bustled behind her making cups of tea, her answer to everything.

'How can he go changing his face? Is that a different face or is he a different person?' she was asking.

'How should I know?' shot back Rose. Then she relented, because that was exactly the question she was asking herself. 'Sorry. The thing is I thought I knew him, Mum. I thought me and him were…'

Neither of them said anything. Rose found she had tears in her eyes.

'And then he goes and does this.' She rubbed her face crossly. 'I keep forgetting he's not human.' To distract herself, she took another pork pie out of the fridge and looked at it. Then she took her mother's sleeve.

'The big question is: where'd you get a pair of men's pyjamas from?'

Jackie shrugged. 'Howard's been staying over.'

'What, Howard from the market? How long's that been going on?'

'A month or so. First of all, he starts delivering to the door and I thought, that's odd. Next thing you know, it's a bag of oranges…'

Rose's attention wandered to the TV next door, which was showing the news. 'Is that Harriet Jones?'

'Oh, never mind me,' said Jackie loudly, but Rose had already headed next door.

Harriet Jones had been the politician who had helped Rose and the Doctor defeat the Slitheen when they'd all been locked inside 10 Downing Street. Rose had adored her, and the Doctor had predicted great things in her future. 'Why's she on the telly?' Rose said, staring at the screen.

'She's Prime Minister now. I'm eighteen quid a week better off. They're calling it "Britain's Golden Age". I keep on saying, my Rose has met her.'

'Did more than that,' said Rose, cheering up. 'Stopped World War Three with her. And now she's PM—Harriet Jones!'

Harriet was giving a speech, and for once, Rose stopped to watch a politician.

'... I don't mean this to sound like a presidential address, but the savings can be implemented by January the 1st. The new Cottage Hospital scheme will be available nationwide from that date, resulting in better healthcare for all. Some might call it radical. I call it vital! And I hope that a great many patients will sleep soundly tonight, as a result—'

The television presenter interrupted.

'Prime Minister, what about those who call the *Guinevere One* space probe a waste of money?'

The Prime Minister looked haughty. 'Now, that's where you're wrong. I completely disagree, if you don't mind. The *Guinevere One* space probe represents this country's limitless ambition: British workmanship sailing up there among the stars.'

Now on screen was a model of a small probe ship. It was a terrible model; Rose squinted at it a bit. They showed how it was moving through space.

'*The unmanned* Guinevere One *is about to begin its final descent,*' said the voiceover. '*Real photographs of the*

Martian landscape should be received back on Earth at midnight tonight.'

Now the TV cut to a press conference, with a sign up above that read BRITISH ROCKET GROUP. The man talking, with his bald head, beard and serious expression, looked old and young at the same time, and the chyron on the screen read DANIEL LLEWELLYN, GUINEVERE PROJECT.

'This is the spirit of Christmas, birth and rejoicing, and the dawn of a new age,' said Llewellyn, 'and that is what we're achieving fifteen million miles away. Our very own miracle…'

Of course, back at the industrial park, they were all watching. The staff had gathered in the communal area—Duerte had tried to rename it the control room, but as it also contained the staff fridge and the tea- and coffee-making facilities, it hadn't caught on. But there was a huge screen hung on the wall, and everyone had gathered round to see their boss on live TV.

A ragged cheer had gone up when he appeared, rapidly hushed so people could listen, but Matthew, Luanne and Duerte were unimpressed.

'He sounds like a massive ponce,' said Duerte.

'I said they should have let me do it,' said Luanne.

'Llewellyn put the team together, directed the operations, oversaw the strategic development *and* let me and Duerte get on with our programming in peace,'

Matthew pointed out. 'I think we should let him have his moment.'

The other two made sucking noises, but everyone fell silent as the screen changed to show the model of their probe again.

Back on the Powell Estate, Jackie glanced at her daughter, who rather looked like she'd had a rug pulled out from under her feet.

'Ever been to Mars?' Jackie asked.

'Nope. God, I feel... Earthbound. They're sending out spaceships—and what about me? I'm stuck at home!'

Jackie rolled her eyes. Rose had been 'stuck at home' for half an hour.

Far, far out, where the cameras didn't show, the little probe was moving; the tiniest dot of light in the vast black nothingness of space, its solar wings spinning gently in the endless night, its own lights displaying the little Union Jack carved in its side on its long, long journey. Llewellyn had insisted on the flag featuring alongside the scientific equipment and a little time capsule of humanity, just in case... It might be a tiny, infinitesimal chance that there was alien life out there, and an even smaller chance that *Guinevere* would bump into them, but if she did...

Beneath the serious exterior, Daniel Llewellyn was a bit of a romantic.

And then the bump came.

Out in the vast wilderness of space, the probe hit something. Something it had not been able to sense; something nobody had known was there; not Matthew, Luanne and Duerte; not Harriet Jones, not Daniel Llewellyn.

Guinevere had hit the side of a giant rock that New Mexico's Very Large Array must have missed; that Jodrell Bank had not even noticed.

And suddenly a panel opened.

This was clearly no ordinary rock. There was something inside it.

White light shone out and the little space probe was sucked inside the great mass of the block of moving granite. And the little door in the rock face slammed shut.

And darkness returned.

5

Here Comes Santa Claus

Rose had decided in the end to leave the Doctor to sleep while she went out with an overexcited Mickey, who wanted to do some Christmas shopping. Oxford Street was busy on Christmas Eve, and Rose couldn't help but find it exciting—yes, obviously the universe was an incredible place, seeing everything they'd seen. But this was something special too. Familiarity. Home. People she loved. And Christmas! She grinned as they passed a brass band all dressed up in Santa Claus outfits, playing a version of 'God Rest Ye Merry Gentlemen'; laughed at the huge decorated tree behind them.

Of course she'd been out of work for months, had never needed any money. She smiled cautiously at Mickey.

'So what do you need? Twenty quid?' he said, reading her mind, as he always could.

'Do you mind? I'll pay you back.'

'Call it a Christmas present.'

Rose took in the heavily decorated surroundings, the people carrying trees, shop windows lit up and the lights everywhere.

'God, I'm all out of sync. You just forget about Christmas and things in the TARDIS. They don't exist. You get sort of timeless.'

Mickey marched on beside her. 'Oh, yeah, that's fascinating, because I love hearing stories about the TARDIS. Oh, go on, Rose, tell us another one because I swear I could listen to it all day. TARDIS this, TARDIS that.'

'Shut up,' said Rose, laughing at him.

'Oh, and one time the TARDIS landed in a big yellow garden full of balloons!'

'I'm not like that!' said Rose, mock-indignant.

'Oh, you so are,' said Mickey.

'Mmm, must drive you mad. I'm surprised you don't give up on me.'

'Oh, that's the thing, isn't it? You can rely on me. I don't go changing my face.'

Rose turned. That one had stung.

'Yeah? What if he's dying?'

'Okay,' said Mickey, looking ashamed of himself.

Rose felt bad for snapping at him and took his hand. 'Sorry.'

Mickey sighed. He missed her so much—missed what they used to be. Missed the future he had once thought they might have. He took a deep breath.

'Just let it be Christmas. Can you do that? Just for a bit. You and me and Christmas. No Doctor, no bog monsters, no life or death.'

'Okay,' said Rose.

'Promise?'

'Yes,' said Rose, and Mickey knew that was the best he was going to get, and he didn't want to risk her dropping his hand again.

'Right! What're you going to get for your mum?'

They wandered down a side street into a Christmas market. 'God Rest Ye Merry Gentlemen' was playing, almost as if they only knew one song.

'I'm round there all the time now, you know,' said Mickey. 'She does my dinner on a Sunday, talks about you all afternoon, yap, yap, yap.'

Rose smiled. Mickey didn't have parents; and her mother would start mothering anyone within a ten-mile radius. She was glad they had each other. Even if she knew her mum was a mean second best to Mickey.

Rose spotted something out of the corner of her eye. It was the band, the brass band dressed up as Santas. Their tin welded masks were actually eerie in the dark, and they...

No. She had been away for too long. It was ludicrous.

They were *not* being followed by a Santa band.

She stared, uneasy, as the creepy bunch moved in front of her and Mickey, holding up their instruments stiffly. The hairs rose on the back of her neck. She looked

39

one straight in the face and it jerked away, quickly, as if to avoid looking at her.

Rose told herself she was being ridiculous. Or was she? Couldn't her travels have left her senses heightened to danger? Mickey was still talking as they walked away; he hadn't noticed a thing. But she wanted to keep an eye on the masked band as the Santas moved towards them, still playing.

She noticed their masks weren't plastic, as she'd imagined they would be. They were metal, a clear hard metal. The fixed smiles looked grotesque painted on to the smooth surfaces. Rose found she couldn't take her eyes off them …

The attack came incredibly fast. The first Santa lifted its trombone and a huge gout of flame blew out from within. Rose screamed Mickey's name, grabbed him and dived to the pavement. Several of the stalls were caught by the blast of flame and immediately started to blaze. The shopping crowds panicked and started charging away. Mickey and Rose got up and crawled behind the nearest stall. The figure with the French horn was slowly raising his weapon.

'It's us!' Rose realised. 'Those Santas are after us!'

Now an electrical stall exploded in front of them; the air was filled with screams and Mickey pulled her away. All of the Santas were lined up now, shooting deadly exploding missiles; following them as they desperately tried to escape down the road. Their tin welded masks looked less like novelties now and more like—could they be some kind of robot?

Rose didn't have time to think as they dived for cover, and stall after stall burst into conflagration all around them.

One of the Santas had them in its sights, fixing them with its painted-on eyes. It lifted its tuba.

As Rose and Mickey froze, paralysed in its sights, the Santa jerked from the recoil as a huge missile hit the enormous Christmas tree in the centre of the plaza. It burst into flame and collapsed immediately on top of the Santa, knocking him over, and giving Rose and Mickey the desperate, precious seconds they needed to make their escape.

They heard the rattling of the tin mask as it fell off to reveal—what? And then they were gone.

'What's going on?' panted Mickey as they ran. 'What've we done? Why are they after us?'

The air was suddenly filled with sirens; police cars and ambulances were screaming past.

'*Taxi!*' Rose waved her arm wildly, as a familiar black cab slowed down, even through the chaos of people charging in front and behind it, and they jumped in.

'They're after the Doctor,' said Rose, then leaned forward. 'I've got to get home. Powell Estate, end of Jordan Road.'

And she pulled out her phone, even as Mickey stared at her, breathless and upset. 'I can't even go shopping with you! We get attacked by a brass band! And who are you phoning?'

'My mum,' said Rose.

'What's she got to do with it?'

'She's in danger!'

Rose willed her mum to pick up but all she could hear on the line was *Beep-beep-beep. Beep-beep-beep.* 'Come on, come on…' She hung up and rang again, hung up and rang again. 'Get off the phone!'

'What were those Santa things?' Mickey asked, still shaking his head.

'I don't know.' Rose stared glumly out of the rear window, where she could just see the flames licking up behind the buildings. 'But think about it. They were after us. What's important about us? Nothing, except the one thing we've got tucked up in bed. The Doctor.'

6

O, Christmas Tree

Back in the flat, Jackie was rabbiting on to her friend Bev in the next block. Jackie liked Bev a lot. Bev had been a hairdresser for thirty-five years, so she did Jackie's roots on the cheap and was a tremendous listener.

While she talked, Jackie made two mugs of tea—one for herself and one for the mystery man asleep in the next room. '… so she turns up, see, no warning. I've got nothing in. I said, Rose, if you want a Christmas dinner of meat paste, then so be it.' She paused, grimaced. 'Oh, no. Don't come round, darling. No, you'd be sorry, flat's all topsy-turvy. Yeah, she just barges in and litters the place. Yeah. No, I'll come round and see you on Boxing Day…'

Bev liked Jackie and didn't like to interrupt her rattling on. She knew how lonely she was. It was hard, knocking about on your own like that. She worried about her. Thank goodness she had Howard now, but even so. There was a limit to how much conversation one could make about grapefruit. So Bev made approving noises as she stirred tomorrow's cranberry sauce; she had her whole noisy, boisterous, loving family arriving in the morning and it was going to be crazy. Nicely crazy, but crazy nonetheless. She found Jackie babbling on curiously restful.

Jackie felt relaxed now, too. She liked to pretend Rose did nothing but annoy her, whilst rubbing it in to her friends that her daughter led an amazing action-packed life of travelling and adventure. The strange man was still asleep in bed, and Jackie left the mug of tea beside it, without pausing for breath. Then she left the room.

Once again, the golden regeneration light emerged from the prone figure, shone in the quiet room, then vanished off into the galaxy...

Rose and Mickey burst into the flat, panting for breath. Jackie was still chatting.

'GET. OFF. THE. PHONE!' Rose shouted.

'It's only Bev. She says hello!' said Jackie.

Rose grabbed it. 'Bev? Yeah. Look. It'll have to wait.' She hung up rudely, and Jackie frowned.

'Right, it's not safe. We've got to go. All of us, and the Doctor, we've got to get out. Where can we go?'

'My mate Stan,' said Mickey. 'He'll put us up.'

Rose gave him one of her looks. 'That's only two streets away. What about Mo? Where's she living now?'

'I don't know. Peak District?' said Jackie.

'Well, we'll go to Cousin Mo's then.'

Jackie stared at her, dumbfounded. 'It's Christmas Eve! We're not going anywhere! What're you babbling about?'

Rose realised that the three of them yelling at each other wasn't going to help matters, and made a determined effort to slow down and lower her voice. 'Mum. Trust me. Someone's after the Doctor. There were these things—they looked like Santa, they had the hats and faces, like they were using all that Christmas stuff as a disguise and…'

She caught a glimpse of something over her mother's shoulder, and stopped short. Something was very wrong.

Rose had spent eighteen Christmases in this flat. Eighteen years of dry turkey and her mum having too much brandy and crying about her dad and getting the photo albums out again. And each year they got out the same old white tree. They would dredge up the tatty paper angels that Rose had made in her first year at school, and the ancient tinsel that got more and more moth-eaten every year… That tree was one of the first things she ever remembered. She knew it as well as she knew her own bed. She'd know it anywhere.

The thing in the corner of the room wasn't their tree.

She lowered her voice further. 'Mum. Where'd you get that? That's a new tree. Where'd you get it?'

Her mother glanced round. The tree in the corner of the room was beautiful: huge and lush and green and perfectly decorated.

'I thought it was you.'

'How can that be me?'

'Well, you went shopping. There was a ring at the door, and there it was!'

Rose's heart was beating faster now and she felt panic steal over her.

'No. That wasn't me.'

'… then who was it?' said Jackie as they all turned to look at it.

Slowly, and ominously, the bottom of the tree lit up, and started playing a tuneless, meandering version of 'Jingle Bells'. Rose could only stare. The next layer of lights went on, and then the next and the next, all the way up to the star at the top.

Rose's voice was a whisper. 'Oh, you're kidding me.'

The tree began to rotate, impossibly, different sections going different ways—and now it was moving forwards, towards them, the branches fast as a buzz saw.

It looked like a joke, as if it were meant to be funny—right up to the second it started to move, the deadly arms moving round at terrible speed. It glanced off the coffee table and tore through it like a woodchipper; tiny sections of razor-sharp wood spitting everywhere, creating a hurricane-like wind in the room.

'Get out!' Mickey shouted to Rose, who had already grabbed her mum. 'Go! *Go!* Get out!' And he bravely picked up a chair, as if fending off a tiger, and stood in front of the wild Christmas tree.

Rose pulled Jackie back towards the bedroom, even as she was opening the front door.

'What are you doing?' screamed Jackie. 'We need to get out!'

'We've got to save the Doctor!' Rose shouted in response. 'We can't just leave him!' Her attention was diverted as the tree started to shred the legs of the chair Mickey was holding. 'Mickey, get out of there!'

He threw the remains of the chair at the tree— which didn't slow it down for an instant—and they all ran for the bedroom.

The tree simply burst into the corridor towards them. Jackie was distraught.

'Leave him,' she screamed about the Doctor. 'Just leave him'– even as the tree broke the internal window in the living room and glass shattered everywhere.

'Get in here,' said Mickey grimly, pulling her with them into the bedroom, and as the tree bore down on her, Jackie did so. She and Mickey pulled a wardrobe across the bedroom door. The awful Christmas music had sped up; the horrible tinny bouncy sound rising over the whir of the branches as the thin plywood of the cheap door began to shred under the onslaught.

The Doctor was still lying there, on his back in the bed, completely unconscious and absolutely oblivious to the commotion happening in the rest of the flat. Jackie was frantic. This was ridiculous.

Despite the urgency of the situation, Rose went towards him and knelt on the bed. 'Doctor, wake up!'

Surely. Surely he'd hear her. Surely, if he was really the Doctor... She leaned over, found his sonic screwdriver in his old jacket pocket and put it in his hand, as the tree went on tearing its way relentlessly through the door.

'I'm going to get killed by a Christmas tree!' shrieked Jackie in fear, now cowering on the floor. She and Mickey had leapt back as the door gave way, and then the wardrobe shattered, and the tree began to spin through the wrecked doorway and into the room.

Rose didn't even look round. She bent down and whispered into the Doctor's ear two words:

'Help me.'

Without warning, the slim figure sat bolt upright and pointed the sonic at the tree—which promptly exploded.

The razor-sharp branches hit the wall like giant darts of fir, one two inches from Jackie's head. She turned to look at it, uncomprehendingly. Now the music and the screaming had stopped, it was suddenly very quiet in the room.

'Remote control!' said the Doctor loudly, immediately awake and alert, and with a fierce expression on his face. 'But who's controlling it?'

7

It Came Upon the Midnight Clear

The Doctor leapt out of bed, pulled on a dressing gown and ran out of the flat. Rose, Mickey and Jackie followed, trying not to look at the devastation.

Rose soon found that she desperately needed the cold, crisp fresh air. Down below, by the bins and the old car up on blocks that hadn't been moved in living memory, stood the sinister figures of the three remaining Santas from the shopping plaza. One was holding a perfectly ordinary-looking remote control, and the strange metal masks turned to look up at them.

'That's them!' said Mickey. 'What are they?'

'Shush,' said Rose. She didn't want to draw attention to them; the way their absolutely normal look had invaded their Christmas; *her* Christmas. And she wanted—needed—to pay attention to somebody else. She needed to see what this new Doctor was doing.

His angular face was cold, his gaze fixed on the Santas below. He raised the sonic as if it was a deadly weapon, gesticulated in a threatening way and the

Santas began to back away, uncertainly. Then he aimed it straight at them, down in the chilly empty courtyard. Immediately, they started to glow blue, then, with a whoosh, teleported away.

Rose stared at the empty car park and thought she should feel less dread. But she didn't. Not at all. She looked at the Doctor and her heart sank. She had thought that that might be it; that he would be better. But in fact he was leaning against the wall; sweating, clearly unwell. She darted to his side.

'They've just gone!' Mickey was saying. 'What kind of rubbish were they? I mean, no offence, but they're not much cop if a sonic screwdriver's going to scare them off.'

'Pilot fish,' said the strange new Time Lord, inexplicably.

'What?' said Rose.

'They were just… pilot fish…' The Doctor collapsed again, gasping in pain.

'What is it? What's wrong?' said Rose.

'You woke me up too soon. I'm still regenerating. I'm bursting with energy.'

He took a sharp deep breath in, then exhaled, and once more the strange golden mist emerged from his mouth; floating, beautiful, incandescent; becoming one with the starry sky. They all watched it go.

'You see? That's it. The pilot fish could smell it a million miles away. So they eliminate the defence—

that's you lot—and they carry me off. They could run their batteries off me for a couple of—'

He collapsed in agony.

'Oh!' said Jackie. 'Oh no!'

'My head,' said the Doctor, anguished. 'I'm having… I'm having a neural implosion. I need…'

They tried to help him inside as he staggered.

'What do you need?' said Jackie.

'I need—'

'Say it. Tell me, tell me, tell me.'

But he couldn't get the words out. 'I need—'

'Painkillers?' offered Jackie

'I need—'

'Do you need aspirin?'

'I need—'

'Codeine? Paracetamol? Oh, I don't know, Pepto-bismol?'

'I need—'

'Liquid paraffin? Vitamic C? Vitamin D? Vitamin E?'

'I need—'

'Is it food? Something simple. Bowl of soup. A nice bowl of soup? Soup and a sandwich? Soup and a little ham sandwich?'

With a tremendous effort of will, the Doctor straightened up his head. 'I need you to shut up!'

Jackie blinked and looked at Rose. 'He hasn't changed that much, has he?'

It was odd, Rose thought. Jackie seemed to have accepted without question what she herself could not manage.

The Doctor tried to stand, fighting the pain. 'We haven't got much time. If there's pilot fish, then'—he withdrew his hand from his pocket in surprise—'why is there an apple in my dressing gown?'

'Oh, that's Howard. Sorry.'

'He keeps apples in his dressing gown?'

'He gets hungry!'

'What, he gets hungry in his sleep?'

'Sometimes!'

Before the Doctor could comment further, he cried out as another huge wave of pain crashed through him, and he sagged to the ground. Rose knelt down with him.

'Brain collapsing. The pilot fish. The pilot fish mean that something, *something...*' He opened his eyes and stared directly at Rose.

'Something... something is coming,' he croaked.

And then he passed out.

Rose put the Doctor back to bed. He was worse. She knew he was worse, although she tried not to think about it. She stared at his face for a long time, and mopped his brow with a clean handkerchief. The strangest of things; everything about him had changed. The nose, which had been a boxer's nose, was now aquiline; the brow not so creased with worry. All that hair. He was as different a man as could be. And yet, oddly, when he had spoken to her mum like that, of all things, she'd seen a glimpse of the person she had known. And then that glimpse was gone.

You strange, strange thing, she thought to herself. She wanted to stay a while, in the dark and the quiet of the bedroom. She took the stethoscope out again, listened; listened again. One of the heartbeats had fallen still. And outside, the pilot fish were circling…

Mickey had managed to fetch his laptop from his flat. He popped his head round the door, saw her face, didn't want to continue, but knew he had to.

'I found it.'

Rose nodded and sighed, not wanting to leave. But she got up and followed him into their sitting room. Jackie had done a pretty good tidying job already, considering.

Mickey sat down, plugging his computer into the phone socket.

'Jackie, I'm using the phone line. Is that all right?'

'Yeah, keep a count of it,' said Rose's mum from the kitchen.

'Pilot fish,' said Mickey. 'I've seen them on telly, hold on, I'll show you…'

He set about the computer. Jackie came through with a cup of tea for Rose.

'Ooh, it's midnight,' she cooed. 'Christmas Day! Any change?'

'He's worse. Just one heart beating,' said Rose quietly, accepting the tea.

They turned their attention to the television. The reporter was standing looking excited in the studio in front of a large picture of the *Guinevere* rocket.

'Well, someone's happy, anyway,' said Jackie.

There had been panic in the lab when *Guinevere* had blacked out on screen. The technicians had completely lost the picture; hadn't a clue what had happened. They'd checked and rechecked the feed, but had found absolutely nothing in the panic. Duerte's head was in his hands. Matthew felt a little tearful. If all their work was to come to nothing or if something incredible was happening and they couldn't get the cameras up…

Luanne was hastily putting together a press release—and briefing Number 10 on reasons they could give if they had to postpone—when suddenly, out of nowhere, the systems were online again. Everybody breathed a sigh of relief. *Guinevere* was where she was meant to be. Her cameras were out, it seemed, but that was all right; when the time came, they could land her remotely and the world would see something then. They really would. The situation was far from ideal, and events had given them all a fright, but it would make a great anecdote in times to come. Or, at least, so Matthew fervently hoped. Duerte kicked back his seat, stuck his feet on the desk and tried to pretend he'd never been remotely freaked out the entire time. It was a Go.

And now Daniel Llewellyn was on television again. Back at the lab they could have left before the blackout; now it was all hands on deck. But Matthew wasn't sure they'd want to go home anyway. It was such a momentous pinnacle of years of work; it felt right that they should all be together, no matter how many frustrated spouses were dealing with overexcited children back at home.

Matthew called his mum and dad, who were staying up late to watch it, full of pride. Even Duerte's family in Portugal had managed to tune in.

Llewellyn was, to say the least, a little uneasy about appearing on television. His throat was dry and he looked very very nervous, but was clearly doing his best.

'Scientists in charge of Britain's mission to Mars have re-established contact with the *Guinevere One* space probe,' said the cheerful reporter. 'They're expecting the first transmission from the planet's surface in the next few minutes.'

The picture cut to Llewellyn. 'Yes, that's right, we are. We're back on schedule. We've received the signal from *Guinevere One*. The Mars landing would seem to be…'

His voice grew slightly more hesitant.

'… an unqualified success.'

'But is it true that you completely lost contact earlier tonight?'

'Yes, we had a bit of a scare,' said Llewellyn, with a forced smile. '*Guinevere* seemed to fall off the scope but it, it was just a blip. Only disappeared for a few seconds… she's fine now, absolutely fine. We're getting the first pictures transmitted live any minute now. I'd better get back to it. Thanks.'

Jackie sniffed. 'Pictures of Mars, they're all the same. Just rocks and dust. Nothing compared to what we've seen.'

Mickey had managed to get the dial-up connection working, and pulled up the website page with a picture of the little fish.

'Here we go. Pilot fish: scavengers, like the Doctor said. Not much of a threat. They're tiny. But the point is, the little fish swim alongside the big fish.'

'Do you mean like sharks?' said Rose.

'Great big sharks. So, what the Doctor means is, now we've had *them*, the pilot fish, any time now we're gonna get…' He clicked onto a picture of a huge, black-eyed, emotionless shark, teeth on display.

A chill struck Rose's heart. *'Something is coming.'* That was the last thing the Doctor had said.

'And here's the image, coming through live ...' The television announcer sounded excited.

'How close is the shark, then?'

'There's no way of telling, but the pilot fish don't swim far from their daddy.'

'So it's close?'

'... direct from the surface of Mars ...'

Jackie wasn't listening to Rose and Mickey. She was transfixed by the TV. Great broken-up blocky pictures were coming through; the reception was terrible.

Rose and Mickey looked up.

'Funny sort of rocks,' said Jackie.

'The first photographs,' intoned the news reader, *'from the surface of the planet ...'*

'That's not rocks,' said Rose in horror, as the image resolved, resolved again, became clearer and clearer, finally showing itself to be—a face.

A frozen image of a face staring into camera, but like no face Rose had ever seen: bright red eyes and a bright red mouth; a goat-shaped skull, but made of jagged, broken bones; a fierce intelligence burning into the camera; long, hideous teeth, as sharp as those of the shark on Mickey's laptop. The something, whatever it was, wore red robes.

Rose moved towards the screen, fingers outstretched. Jackie and Mickey both kept staring at it. The alien face seemed to be frozen; and then suddenly the image moved, the red eyes flashed and it roared, and bared its huge teeth, straight down the lens of the camera.

8

I Saw Three Ships

All of the television channels had switched to rolling news immediately.

'*The face of an alien life form was transmitted live tonight—on BBC One,*' said the man on the BBC. On AMNN, Trinity Wells was talking about how the human race had been shown absolute proof that alien life existed. There wasn't a channel that was not broadcasting the astonishing discovery.

A long line of sleek black cars sped through the night, arriving in front of the Tower of London. Following the horrifying video, Daniel Llewellyn had been summonsed and he was very, very concerned. This wasn't... Well.

This hadn't been expected at all.

A scientist all his life, part of him couldn't help but be incredibly excited by the discovery. Oh sure, there'd been rumours; whispers. But a real, undeniable alien! And he was right in the heart of the action!

He took a deep breath. Stay calm, Llewellyn, he told himself. Stay calm.

A secret service officer opened the door for him, and he was greeted by a tall, serious-looking army officer leading a troop of Red Berets.

'This way, sir,' said the man, who appeared to be in charge, and Daniel Llewellyn entered the great citadel; the edifice that had protected Britain for hundreds of years, and which was now the base for one of the most ambitious organisations the world had ever known: UNIT.

UNIT, the Unified Intelligence Task Force, was an internationally funded covert military operation set up after the Second World War both to oppose alien threats to humanity and to stop those threats from becoming public knowledge and causing mass panic. It functioned all over the world, and its UK base had recently been moved to one of the most secure citadels on Earth—the Tower of London. Or rather, nine storeys beneath the Tower of London.

If you have ever taken a London Underground train, had to change at Bank station, and wondered why it is such an infernal mess, be assured there's a good reason. Much of the Tube had to be rerouted to accommodate the vast secret network of workshops and vaults fanning out from far below Tower Hill. If you are ever feeling brave, try opening one of the

Monument tunnel doors and see how long it takes the deceptively sleepy-looking London Underground guard to wrestle you to the ground.

The Doctor had worked with UNIT often, and was a close friend of its now-retired head, Brigadier Lethbridge-Stewart. Major Blake, who had greeted Llewellyn, was the current ranking officer: a good man with a serious mind.

But the Doctor had hated the move to Tower Hill. It never failed to remind him of a night, long ago. A freezing, starlit London dark lit only by torches, when he had rowed, in silence, a young, beautiful, utterly terrified woman, her skin fair as milk, trembling in anguish, through Traitor's Gate.

He'd had a plan to save her. It had failed, and she had never seen the sun rise beyond the Tower's walls again, and he could never see the building without hearing the plashing of his oars in the dark water; the muted sobbing; the deathly rattle of the portcullis chains.

Daniel Llewellyn had never heard of UNIT. But he knew one thing: this was the most astonishing thing that had ever happened to him or, in his opinion, any Lampeter graduate.

And now, regardless of the grave task that lay ahead of him—he expected, even as his heart sank to his boots, that important scary people were going to want answers from him that he simply didn't have—he wanted more time, to take in every detail of his clandestine journey; to appreciate the mechanics behind the astonishing lift that silently whisked them down from an unnoticed corridor behind the gift shop. It plummeted at a rate of knots then slid open upon a vast room marked Basement Level 11. Daniel found himself plunged into a vast centre of activity, of important-looking people rushing about, and an atmosphere of very serious focus.

'You've got better facilities than us!' he said at last. 'I spend all that time asking for funds for space exploration and you've built your own Mission Control! How long's all this been here?'

Major Blake barely glanced at him.

'I'm sorry, all information is on a need-to-know basis.'

'Have you been monitoring us?'

'Every step of the way.'

'But… what for?' asked Llewellyn.

'Just in case,' said Major Blake. 'And, as it turns out, we had good reason. If you'd like to come through…'

Llewellyn followed him into the small room, still desperately looking around him.

He found himself in a dark office made entirely of glass panels, overlooking Mission Control. A number of monitors were running, all of them showing the alien roar on a loop.

Standing in the room was the Prime Minister.

Llewellyn felt like he'd fallen down a rabbit hole. Harriet Jones looked concerned, but fundamentally in control; her hair and suit were neat, her posture intense. She was smaller than she looked on television. There was another man in the room; young, with a headset attached to his ear.

'Mr Llewellyn, ma'am.'

The PM, rather surprisingly, immediately took out her ID and showed it to him. 'Harriet Jones. Prime Minister.'

Llewellyn was rather taken aback at that. 'Oh. Well. Yes. I know who you are. I was just saying, quite a place you've got here. I wish you'd give my lot this much support.'

The Prime Minister fixed him with a glance. 'Hardly the time to criticise me.'

He winced. 'No, sorry… I suppose I've ruined your Christmas.'

'Never off duty,' said Harriet, and Llewellyn could well believe it; he was glad he'd voted for her. 'Now, we've put out a cover story. Alex has been handling it.'

The young man with the headset in the corner stepped forward and indicated the monitor. 'We've said it was a hoax. Some sort of mask or prosthetics. Students hijacking the signal, that kind of thing.'

'Alex is my right-hand man,' explained Harriet. 'I'm not used to having a right-hand man. I quite like it, though.'

'I quite like it myself,' said Alex, smiling.

'I don't suppose there's any chance it *was* a hoax?' said Llewellyn.

'That would be nice,' said Harriet. 'Then we could all go home. But there was an incident, this afternoon, in Central London, you might have heard about it?'

'Yes, something to do with a brass band? And a freak storm?'

'Another one of our stories,' sniffed Harriet. 'Maybe not the best, most of the staff's on holiday.'

'Then what was it?'

'Some sort of… skirmish. I don't suppose anyone's offered you a coffee?'

'Um, no.'

To Daniel's astonishment, the Prime Minister of Great Britain started to make him a coffee from the filter machine in the corner.

'Milk?'

'Yes, thanks, just milk.' Llewellyn didn't take milk at all, but he was terribly flustered.

Harriet brought it over. 'Alex, can I get you a cup?'

'No, I'm fine,' said Alex, rather more nonchalant. He was obviously used to such attention.

64

'My grandfather,' Harriet announced abruptly, handing Llewellyn the mug, 'was a bit of a wild card. Spent quite a few years in Venezuela, tried to buy a gold mine, lost every penny.

'But he would tell us all sorts of stories. Adventures. Tales of rebel factions, coming down from the mountains and raiding the townships. He always knew when a raid was being planned, because of the skirmishes.'

She took a step closer, her voice low. 'In the days before an assault there would be, just, little incidents, small scale, thefts and looting. Opportunists, making the most of it, before the proper attack.

'And it's the same with aliens visiting this planet. We get small incidents at first, suggesting something bigger is approaching.'

Llewellyn stared at his coffee, trying not to overreact.

'You seem to be talking about aliens as a matter of fact.'

Harriet Jones smiled rather wickedly in a way that made her look years younger.

'There's an Act of Parliament banning my autobiography.'

Major Blake cleared his throat, looking serious. 'Prime Minister?'

'I'm with you.' Harriet left with him, and beckoned Llewellyn to follow.

Back in the basement, he looked around in wonder. A whole new world ... why on Earth were they not working on the space programme together? The things they could do! He couldn't wait to tell Matt and Duerte... if permitted, of course.

It struck him that Luanne probably knew all this already. It struck him slightly more slowly that the reason they'd thought Luanne never did anything was that she wasn't actually working for them at all, and he winced a little at his naivety. But there wasn't time to think about that now; they were headed into another space, filled with expensive computer equipment and staff deep in concentration. A young woman looked up as they approached.

Sally Jacobs, the young woman at the desk, had been surprised where she'd ended up. Of course the army didn't give you much say. And London was better than, say, Afghanistan. Although she would have quite liked Belize. Even so, having to tell people her job was more or less looking after Beefeaters was a little demeaning.

Still. She got on pretty well with Luanne, her colleague at *Guinevere One*. It was going to be pretty difficult to explain how she was missing Christmas again, though. She thought Rob was probably coming to the end of his tether with her. Well, she'd deal with that in the New Year, because...

She was surprised to see the Prime Minister turn up without security in advance; and surprised to see how tall Daniel Llewellyn was. He looked much better than his file picture, she found herself thinking… Then She collected herself, and jumped up, trying to look as professional as possible. This was big, she thought to herself. This wasn't Beefeaters.

Sally pasted on a small smile as she stood up for the Prime Minister and her team. Major Blake nodded towards her. He was the best boss she'd ever had, by miles.

'Miss Jacobs can explain.'

Sally stepped forward, but before she could begin Harriet put out her hand.

'We haven't met. Harriet Jones, Prime Minister.'

That would have normally put Sally off her stride, but she'd been very well briefed as to how modest Harriet was.

'Yes, I know who you are.' Sally wished her mum could see her now. She took a deep breath and spoke slowly. It was hard to remember in UNIT sometimes that there were people out there—even people like Daniel Llewellyn, working in space exploration—who didn't know what was out there; who hadn't even imagined it. Speaking slowly usually helped. 'So. It turns out, the transmission didn't come from the surface of Mars.'

There was silence as they let this sink in.

'*Guinevere One* was broadcasting from a point five thousand miles above the planet.'

'In other words,' added Major Blake, 'that screaming alien has got a ship; and the probe is on board.'

Llewellyn blinked, astonished. 'But, then they might not be from Mars itself. Maybe they're not actual Martians.'

'Of course they're not,' said Major Blake. 'Martians look completely different. We think the ship was in flight and they just came across the probe.'

'And they're moving,' added Sally, studying Llewellyn to see how he was taking this news for the first time. He was blinking rapidly; you could almost see his brain rearranging itself to this new reality. She remembered when she first found out. She'd been only 22. She had held it together for half an hour, then gone and burst into tears in the toilet. She made her voice as gentle and unthreatening as she could.

'The ship's still in flight now. We've got it on the Hubble Array.'

She pointed to the screen behind her. A dot could be seen on the radar. A moving dot. It was strange quite how ominous that tiny bleep could sound. Llewellyn gazed at it, hypnotised.

'Moving in which direction?' said Harriet quickly.

'Towards us.'

'How fast?'

'Very fast.'

'What was your name again?'

'Sally.'

'Thank you, Sally.'

Harriet looked very, very worried, as the blip continued to move across the radar screen.

9

Hark! The Herald Angels Sing

Rose could hear drunk lads singing in the distance as she crossed the concourse to the flat, carrying two plastic bags. A light blipped overhead and she looked up, terrified. But it was only an aeroplane, passing on its way.

Safely inside, Rose was glad to find that Jackie was still at the Doctor's bedside. 'Right then, let's get him fixed. I went to the all-night chemist. Got every kind of medicine off the shelf.'

Rose emptied the bags: cough medicine, lotions and ointment.

'We've got to try them all, dab a bit on him, see if he reacts—he said he needed something, maybe some sort of chemical. For all we know it's one of these.'

'I made a start,' said Jackie proudly, holding up a bottle.

Rose squinted.

'But that's shampoo!'

'Contains ZTP!' said Jackie

'Rose!' shouted Mickey from the other room. Rose got up reluctantly, gave her mum a stern look. 'Just be sensible, OK?'

In the living room, Mickey was typing up a storm on his laptop. The first time Rose had met Harriet Jones, in Downing Street when that Raxacoricofallapatorius business had kicked off, the Doctor had helped Mickey, a keen amateur hacker, by using his sonic screwdriver on the computer to speed it up and make everything a bit easier. Afterwards, he had completely forgotten to remove this ability. Mickey wasn't complaining; he used it mostly to win eBay auctions but had never lost sight of its potential.

Which meant that, despite UNIT's exceptional levels of international standard encryption security, thanks to Mickey's Sony VAIO with 512mb of RAM, Mickey, Sally, Daniel Llewellyn, Major Thomas Blake and the Prime Minister of Great Britain were all watching exactly the same feed, staring at the same picture: the blip, travelling through space.

'Rose! Take a look! I've got access to the military!'

'The Doctor told you to wipe it!' said Rose.

'Yeah, yeah. But look, though, they're tracking a spaceship. It's big, it's fast and it's coming this way.'

'Coming for what, though?' said Rose, peering at the screen. 'The Doctor?'

'Dunno, but... it's like with all that fish stuff. The big fish doesn't even know the pilot fish exist. The big fish is just hungry. The big fish eats. So maybe it's coming for all of us.'

'How long till it gets here?' said Rose, her insides chilled. The Doctor had to wake up. He had to.

'It's almost too fast to follow,' said Mickey. 'But not too long at this rate.'

There was a bleep, then some interference on the monitor.

'Hold on.' Mickey stared at the screen. 'The ship— it's transmitting.'

Harriet, Llewellyn and the team were staring at the big screen, in awe; the picture resolved, slowly through the pixels once again.

Harriet felt nervous, but slightly excited. This country was her responsibility now, and she was glad she wasn't coming to a business like this fresh. Even so, she wished she knew where the Doctor was.

Llewellyn was utterly gripped; terrified and elated at the same time. One of the biggest disappointments in his life had come when he'd started studying physics and engineering, and realised the limitations on space travel made it very unlikely that his generation would ever encounter extraterrestrial intelligence. He'd hoped against hope that some day in his lifetime contact might be made, but he was not expecting it. So Llewellyn was not as apprehensive as the others; his awe was too overwhelming. He realised his mouth was hanging open, and that the girl, Sally, might have noticed it, so he shut it quickly and tried to convey a nonchalance he absolutely did not feel. About anything.

This time there were four aliens on the screen. Their bodies looked big, and bulky; a stranger outline than human, but swathed in red robes, and covered in what looked like pieces of bone. They had whips and swords around their waists like warriors, and the one at the front—the leader, presumably—was talking. Although it sounded more like snarling; like the growling of wolves.

'*GATZ TA KA TAAAAA!!!!*' screamed the voice. '*KA SOO ME FADROC. KA SOO ME SYCORAX! KASH KACK PALHAA ME NO SO COVNA! BASSIC CODRAFEE PEL HUSTA! CODRAFEE MEL SO TOR!!!!*'

'Have you seen them before?' Mickey was asking Rose back in the flat, but she shook her head in horror. 'No!'

'*SO PEDRA CAY! SO PANDACK! SOO MASSAC REL BEECRO, COL CHACK CHII! SYCORA JAK! SYCORA TELPO! SYCORA FAA!!*'

'Translation software,' ordered Major Blake at UNIT control, and Alex immediately moved towards the door. 'Yes, sir.'

All of the aliens joined in with the figure on the screen, screaming furiously. *'SYCORA JAK!! SYCORA TELPO! SYCORA FAAA!!!!'*

Staring at the hacked UNIT feed, Rose couldn't get her head around it.

'I don't understand what they're saying,' she said, in despair. 'The TARDIS translates alien languages inside my head, all the time, wherever I am.'

'So why isn't it doing it now?' asked Mickey.

'I don't know. Must be the Doctor. Like he's part of the circuit, and he's, he's broken...'

Her face was desolate.

'He's not just sick... he's gone.'

10

In the Bleak Midwinter

Major Blake and the Prime Minister found a corner in which to converse privately.

'I'm getting demands from Washington, ma'am. The President's insisting that he take control of the situation.'

Harriet Jones raised her eyebrows. 'You can tell the President, and please use these exact words: He's not my boss, and he's certainly not turning this into a war.'

'With respect, ma'am. For all your experience, you haven't handled anything like this before.'

'With respect, Major,' said Harriet Jones. 'Who has?'

She moved quickly towards Alex, who was busy with the translation software on his laptop; he was playing the alien message on a loop. It sounded even more threatening when repeated over and over.

'What have we got?'

'Nothing yet. Translating an alien language is like cracking a code: it's going to take time.'

'For all we know, that was a message of peace,' said Major Blake. 'How far off is this ship?'

'About five hours,' said Alex.

Harriet rubbed her forehead with her hands. Five hours. The countdown had already begun, it seemed. And they did not understand yet whether they were friend or foe. This was worse than her first Prime Minister's Questions.

She thought about homes across the land; children overexcited—up already? Oh no, they were surely fast asleep, dreaming of sugar plums—it was the night before Christmas: but something *was* stirring.

And it was Harriet's job to protect them; every one. And she didn't have the faintest idea where to start, if Alex and the good people at UNIT—the cleverest they had; the cleverest anybody had—couldn't crack the code.

She needed more tea. And oh my goodness, she had to call her mother; the poor love would be terrified.

Even now AMNN was reporting that NATO forces were on red alert.

Jackie was kneeling by the Doctor's bed. 'Come on sweetheart,' she cooed. 'What do you need?'

But the figure didn't stir.

Mickey was listening to the transcript of the alien conversation, trying a few things, but getting absolutely nowhere. It was four o'clock in the morning. Christmas morning. Never mind Santa's sleigh, here was a ship full of aliens on its way; did they come in heavenly peace, or to tear open the Earth like a present under the tree, and throw the wrapping away?

He thought about everyone he knew; Stevo's kids from down the garage who couldn't stop talking about the PlayStation they were going to get, whilst Stevo said of course they wouldn't, they hadn't behaved themselves, all the time smiling fondly, and Mickey knew he'd had it wrapped and hidden behind the tyres for three weeks.

On the television behind him, the newsreader said, seriously, *'People are calling this... our longest night...'*

What was the morning going to bring? He felt terrified and alone. He glanced around for Rose. She wasn't there.

Rose had gone in to watch the Doctor who lay still as a carved knight on a tomb. Jackie had fallen asleep in the chair next to the bed, all the useless medicines scattered around her.

Rose looked at her watch: it was 5 a.m. now. And still no change.

Five miles north, Daniel Llewellyn sat on the stone steps of the embankment in front of the Tower of London, just at the base of the famous bridge. Dawn was breaking. It looked like being a perfect, blue-skied, winter's day.

Daniel heard footsteps behind him; it was the UNIT staffer, Sally Jacobs. She smiled rather anxiously at him, and he made to stand up politely before she shooed him down again, then half-returned the grin.

'Nothing yet?'

'Nothing yet,' she agreed, holding out a coffee.

'I didn't add any milk,' she said.

'Well. Well, that's kind,' said Daniel, taking it as she moved to sit down on the step beside him. 'So you've had us under surveillance?'

'Yes, sorry. It does rather blight getting to know someone.'

He looked at her, and they smiled, nervously, at one another.

'What do you think will happen?' he said. 'I mean, I'm guessing you've been through this kind of thing before.'

Sally blinked, not wanting to give away too much, nor to give false hope. Not that there was much about, since there was another fly in the ointment: UNIT control was trying to get in touch with their old ally, the Doctor (she had never met him, but she had heard

80

an awful lot about him). So far, they didn't appear to have had much luck.

Llewellyn noted her reticence immediately.

'It's all right,' he said. 'I've been telling people I've been working on washing machines for the last four years.'

She smiled at that and they shared a moment of understanding. He warmed his hands around the cup she'd brought him; she found she was twirling a lock of her hair round her fingertips. As soon as she realised she was doing it, she abruptly stopped. He noticed her stopping and blinked.

Sally jumped up. This was ridiculous. She moved towards the water, looking all around; shivering in the cold.

'Gorgeous, isn't it?' she said, just for something to say. The sun was slowly rising above London's latest half-built skyscraper: a rocket-shaped structure that UNIT had ordered be nicknamed 'the Gherkin' in case people got any ideas of what they were planning to build inside it; above the gleaming spires of the Tower, bouncing off the sparkling Thames all the way down the bend of the river to Westminster.

All Llewellyn could see were the rays dancing off the gold of Sally's hair. It was Christmas morning. It might, Llewellyn thought suddenly, be the last dawn he'd ever see. And yet, somehow, out here in the silence of an empty city, alone with a beautiful girl, he somehow wasn't quite as scared as he might have been.

Rose was still standing in the doorframe, staring in. Mickey joined her. He felt washed out.

'Hey.'

'How are you getting on?'

Mickey's attempts to decode the alien language had come to nothing. 'I can't even translate French,' said Mickey sadly. 'Christmas morning. Everyone'll be waking up. Opening their presents. No idea what's coming.'

'Even his voice changed,' said Rose, following a different line of thought.

Mickey looked at her. 'Yeah, that's our biggest problem right now.'

'How can he change his accent, though?'

'Well, you pick up accents, don't you? Depending who you're with. Depending who you're close to.'

His voice was quiet.

'Maybe he got it off you.'

Rose was shaking her head. 'But the Doctor wouldn't do this. The old Doctor. The proper Doctor. He'd wake up. He'd save us.'

She moved in to Mickey and laid her head on his shoulder.

'Oh, I like that,' said Mickey. 'He's let you down, so I get all the hugs.'

Nothing marked Mickey so well in the war—his own war, the only one he was never, ever going to win—as the manner in which he took his defeats.

'You really love him, don't you?' he said. But he stood strong and he took the sobbing, and the hugging, until morning came.

11

Walking in the Air

UNIT was never fully quiet; people were still working and on duty, efficient and chilly as the atmosphere. Major Blake was sitting alone, as Harriet approached him. She glanced around, but there was nobody close.

'I don't suppose we've had a Code Nine?' she murmured. 'No sign of the Doctor?'

'Nothing yet,' said Blake. 'You've met him, haven't you? I've only seen the classified files. More like the stuff of legend.'

'He is that.' She sighed. 'Failing him, what about Torchwood?'

Blake stuttered. 'Well. I- I don't really think…'

'I know I'm not supposed to know about it, I realise that. But if ever we needed Torchwood, it's now…'

'Nothing's been tested!'

'Then I suggest they start,' said Harriet.

The Major shook his head. 'I can't take responsibility.'

'I can. See to it. Get them ready.'

The Major hesitated, only for an instant. Then he got up and walked off, his mouth a grim line.

Harriet sagged in her seat, and just for an instant the full weight of the office passed over her brow.

'Prime Minister?'

It was Alex. There was something about his youthful face and boundless enthusiasm for hard work that made her forget her own fatigue.

She forced herself upright. 'Has it worked?'

'Just about,' said Alex. He pressed the button again, and the growling tape played. He talked over it at the same time.

'"*People*"—that could be cattle. "*You belong to us. To the Sycorax.*" They seem to be called Sycorax, not Martians. "*We own you. We now possess your land, your minerals, your precious stones. You will surrender or they will die. Sycorax strong, Sycorax mighty, Sycorax rock.*" As in the modern sense, they rock.'

Llewellyn and Sally had reappeared for this and now stood close together. They looked at one another, their worst fears confirmed.

Llewellyn, who'd been regarding the monitor quietly, lifted his head. 'They will die? Not *you* will die, *they* will die? Who's "they"?'

'I don't know,' said Alex, 'but it is the right personal pronoun. It's "they".'

Harriet's face was set in a grim mask. 'Can we send a message back?'

86

'Can we do that?' Alex asked Sally, who nodded. 'If they're listening, yeah,' and Llewellyn glanced at her, impressed.

'Then send them a reply. Tell them: This is a day of peace on planet Earth. Tell them, we extend that peace to the Sycorax.'

Alex was typing it in.

'Then tell them: This planet is armed... and we do not surrender.'

Mickey was watching it all from the front room.

'You'd better come and see this!' he shouted to Rose, who was washing her hair.

'Aliens online.'

The four Sycorax appeared again, in a diamond formation this time, with one—the leader, Llewellyn supposed, watching on the huge screen at UNIT– standing up.

The creature walked towards the probe camera, and held up his hands. His fingers were bony; skeletal, with only skeins of skin between them. He opened his palm out to the camera. And then his fingers just flicked out. Flicked out towards them, again and again, in small jerky movements, and glowed blue. And suddenly Llewellyn could see a little blue light dancing around his fingers; fluttering around, the tiniest bobbing light.

And then the image fizzed out in reverse, and cut dead, and was gone.

The room looked round in puzzlement.

'What was that?' Harriet was still staring at the monitor. 'Was that a reply?'

'I don't know… It looked like some kind of energy or… static?' suggested Alex.

'Maybe it's a different form of language, some sort of ideogram or pictogram or…' Llewellyn looked straight at Harriet. 'It looked to me like they were casting a spell.'

Llewellyn was the first to spot it, as Sally Jacobs suddenly got a glazed look on her face and headed for the exit. Blue light was dancing over her head, as it was over many others in the room. As if to a prearranged signal, they all got up, as one, and followed her.

'What the hell? It's the light! It's the same light!' He caught sight of Sally moving away. 'Sally, what are you doing? Sally?'

Daniel attempted to pull her back, but she pushed on and kept on going; she could not be stopped. She didn't even react, continued walking. Her eyes were open; she wasn't bumping into things. But it was as if she were sleepwalking, as if she were in a completely different world to him, utterly indifferent.

'Let go of her, you'll hurt her!' said Harriet, and Llewellyn dropped Sally's arm like it was hot. The soldiers at the door raised their guns—although several of them had left their posts and were walking, like Sally, as if in their sleep, but the Major ordered them to stand down immediately.

'Let them pass!' ordered Blake.

'But where are they going?' said Alex, as they watched the sleepwalkers move onward in utter, eerie silence, as if a spell had been cast upon them. He began to follow.

Back in the industrial park, stuck in his wheelchair, of course, Matthew couldn't chase Duerte up the stairs.

Okay, they'd had a long night trying to get someone to tell them what was up; trying to get Daniel to answer his bloody phone, which appeared to be blocked. But even so, he'd never known Duerte sleepwalk before. And not just him—loads of people around here were doing the same. They'd turned into zombies.

And the light. That weird light flickering over them, the like of which he'd never seen before.

Helplessly Matthew screamed up after Duerte. 'Come back! Come down! What's wrong, don't you want to eat my brains?'

But the figures were blank, and removed, and didn't stop, or turn around, and Matthew could only watch as they got higher, and higher up the stairs, and finally disappeared from view.

Jason Overton from the laundrette, his face completely blank, walked right past Jackie's front door, pursued by a frantic woman crying, 'What's wrong with you? Jason? Jason!'

Rose heard the commotion and came out. She recognised her neighbour immediately.

'Sandra?'

'He won't listen. He's just walking. He won't stop walking! There's this sort of light thing…'

The pale blue glow was flickering over his head.

'Jason? Stop it right now! Please Jason, just stop!'

Rose looked down and caught her breath. Right through the estate, like zombies, wearing pyjamas or half-dressed, were dozens of people. Pursuing them anxiously were friends and families, begging them to stop, trying to pull them back. It was no use: those affected seemed like robots, their pace relentless.

Rose's heart sank. The sharks were getting nearer.

At UNIT too the full extent of the invasion—or infection, or whatever it was—was becoming clear, as Harriet, Alex and Llewellyn rushed out to follow the blank-eyed marchers.

'They're all heading in the same direction,' Harriet pointed out.

'It's only certain people. Why isn't it affecting us?' said Llewellyn.

Alex hung up his phone with a grim look on his face. 'Prime Minister, reports are coming in. The same thing is happening all over the country. There are thousands of people affected—maybe millions—and nobody knows how or why!'

12

Angels We Have Heard on High

It wasn't just all over the country. It was all over the world. Desperate families were running beside blank-staring, zombified men, women and children, all of them taking stairs, or escalators, or pressing into lifts, heading in the same direction—up.

From the Tower of London to the Coliseum in Rome, from the Taj Mahal to Sydney Harbour Bridge: as if hypnotised, fathers and sons, mothers and daughters walked steadily onward, all pursued by their increasingly desperate and hysterical loved ones. If pulled to the ground, they would fight back with superhuman strength, until they made their way free, then simply carry on. If they were locked in rooms, they would break out; if locked in cells, they would walk in the same direction, banging their heads off the walls, scraping their fingernails down to nothing trying to get out. Babies were abandoned by the side of the road or, if screaming to reach one direction, picked up and carried along with everyone else. The mothers were frantic.

They marched, a great, hypnotised silent, eerie army of humanity; from every town, from every village and city, to the highest point near to them. They were heading for their nearest high-rise building. Anything with stairs, anything with steps. Fire escapes. Towers. Castles. Skyscrapers. Onwards, they marched relentlessly, onto the roofs; slow moving feet clanging on fire escapes. Right to the very edges of the roofs, poised on a hundred million precipices.

And then they stopped.

Llewellyn followed Sally up to the top of the Tower of London, the city spread below. She stood there, in a line with all the others, frozen, like a robot. A policeman was reporting just below them. 'They've gone right to the edge. They're going to jump. They're all going to jump!'

Daniel didn't pull or grab, but he very gently took her hand. She did not feel it, or if she did, she gave no sign. It felt as cold as ice. He looked at it.

'Sally, just listen. Just stop,' said Llewellyn in his calmest voice. 'It's Daniel Llewellyn. Danny. Sally, just concentrate. Listen to me. We need you. Stop this, Sally!'

Daniel's phone rang and he stood back to answer it, unable to take his eyes off the girl, her hair streaming in the wind; not looking quite human any longer, but like something feral waiting to take flight.

Alex from downstairs was calling. His voice was scared and low.

'According to reports it's a third. One-third of the world's population. That's two billion people ready to jump.'

Llewellyn looked at the girl on the ledge, and he didn't have to even think of all the people balanced on top of the pyramids of Egypt; the people teetering on the windy fretwork of the Eiffel Tower; he didn't have to think about everyone. He had to think about one person, and he didn't hesitate.

'We have to surrender, then,' he said. 'Surrender or they'll die.'

Rose and Mickey stood at the very top of their building. They stared out, taking in the sight of every tower block roof in South London, as far as the eye could see, lined with human silhouettes. All the way across the river to the buildings in the city; each precipice a cluster of dark human shapes like flies on fruit.

'It's an invasion,' said Mickey, his blood well and truly chilled. 'Different way of invading, gotta give them that, but all the same. What do we do?'

Rose's face was stony. 'Nothing we *can* do. There's no one to save us. Not any more.'

Harriet was demanding answers. Llewellyn had descended. He could do nothing upstairs; perhaps he could be more useful in Mission Control.

But he hated leaving Sally behind. He'd called his parents; they were fine. But the neighbours—the mother and the little girl had gone, just walked out of the house on a freezing morning, in their pyjamas. His mother's voice was grey with anxiety; she pleaded with her son to come home.

'I can't, Mam. I'm trying to… I'm trying to help out here.'

'With this? What's it got to do with washing machines, *bach*?'

'Just stay inside, Mam. I'll… I'll be home when I'm able.'

'All right. Merry Christmas, yes?'

Llewellyn found he was unable to respond and, swallowing heavily, gave himself a second, hung up, then turned round, shaking his head.

'Why are only some people affected?' he said dismally. 'Why not us?'

Alex was desperately leafing through the file reports coming in, and listening to his headset.

'Wait a minute. There might be some kind of pattern. All these people tend to be father and son, mother and daughter, brothers and sisters. Family groups, but not so often husbands and wives.'

Llewellyn blinked for a second. That reminded him of something. 'Some sort of genetic link, but…'

Then it came to him in a flash. 'Oh my God. It's *Guinevere One*. These people, do we know what blood

96

group they are? No, wait a minute, have you got medical records on file? For all your staff?'

'Of course we have, yes,' said Alex, starting to rise. 'But why—?'

'I need to see them.' Llewellyn grabbed Alex by the arm and steered him towards the main doors. 'Now.'

And they left, Llewellyn hoping that his hunch wasn't true. But he feared, with a horrible stone of certainty in his stomach, that it was. And if that was the case, then this entire thing was all his fault.

'What about Torchwood?'

Harriet Jones asked the question straight out. Major Blake still didn't like the word being spoken aloud. Things between the two agencies were… well, 'delicate' to say the very least. And something like this stepped right across all the lines; tore through the Chinese walls. He glanced left and right and lowered his voice.

'Still working on it. Bear in mind they have just lost a third of their staff too.'

'But do they have what we need?'

Blake looked her in the eyes, unflinching. 'Yes, ma'am.'

'Then, for God's sake, tell them to hurry up.'

Daniel Llewellyn, perspiring slightly, logged in to the database in the records room, helped by a scared-looking member of staff. Personal UNIT files were guarded like gold.

'Here it is. Sally Jacobs, blood group A positive.' His heart was pounding. 'Who else walked out?'

'Luke Parsons,' said Alex, glancing up.

Llewellyn typed his name in. 'Luke Parsons. A positive.'

'Jeffrey Baxter.'

'Baxter. A positive. That's it. They're all A positive. Can you call your boss?'

Harriet and the Major arrived in an instant, and Llewellyn explained the situation.

'How many people in the world are A positive?' asked Blake.

'No idea, but I'll bet it's one-third,' said Llewellyn.

'What's so special about that blood group?'

'Nothing.' Llewellyn sat up slowly and blew air through his mouth. This was the moment he'd been dreading. 'It's my fault.' Sighing heavily, he turned round to face them, his face distraught. '*Guinevere One*. It's got one of those plaques identifying the human race. A message to the stars. I mean, it's standard form, really; you don't expect anything to come of it, but I put on maps and music and samples… There's wheat seeds, and water, and… and… blood.'

'Whose?' Harriet demanded.

'It's Duerte's, one of the tech guys—A positive.' Llewellyn swallowed heavily and stared at the floor.

'I hate needles—I was too cowardly to use my own blood. And now, the Sycorax have got a vial of A positive blood, and, well, I don't know how, but through that…'

'They're controlling one-third of the human population,' said Harriet quietly.

Llewellyn sank his head in guilt. 'I put the blood on board. Oh my God.'

Harriet stepped forward and patted him on the shoulder. 'Don't blame yourself. You couldn't possibly have known. And if you'd chosen blood from the O group we'd have *half* the population out there.' She turned to leave the room. 'Major! With me. There's only one more thing I can try…'

13

Silent Night

Rose and Mickey went back to the flat. They didn't know what else to do. Rose felt thoroughly defeated. The telly was still blaring.

'It's on telly, they're saying it's everyone!' said Jackie, rushing up to them. 'Whole planet. People just standing on the edge, there's two thousand people on the White Cliffs of Dover...'

Suddenly the television went black, and the words EMERGENCY BROADCAST appeared on screen.

Harriet Jones sat behind a large wooden desk, two large Union Jacks and a Christmas tree behind her. She glanced to check the TV cameras were on, then turned to address the nation.

'Ladies and gentlemen... if I may take a moment during this terrible time? It's hardly the Queen's speech, I'm afraid that's been cancelled.'

A thought suddenly occurred to her and she glanced off-screen.

'Did we ask about the Royal Family?'

Alex responded by immediately jabbing a finger upwards.

'Oh. They're on the roof.' Harriet cleared her throat. 'All of them?' At his nod, she took a deep breath. 'Ladies and gentleman, this crisis is unique, and I very much fear there might be worse to come. I would ask all of you to remain calm. But I have one request: Doctor. If you're out there. We need you.'

On the Powell Estate, Jackie turned to glare at Rose and Mickey. Harriet's voice blared on out of the television screen.

'I don't know what to do. But if you can hear me, Doctor. If anyone knows the Doctor—'

Rose turned away, her heart breaking.

'—if anyone can find him—the situation has never been more desperate.'

Rose walked slowly down the corridor to the Doctor's room, tears cascading down her cheeks.

'... help us, please, Doctor. Help us.'

Rose leaned against the doorframe, sobbing like a child as she watched the form of this man who was not the real Doctor, not any more, still in the bed. The brand new face of her loss.

Everything in her life had fallen apart so very quickly, it had vanished beneath her feet; everything she had; everything she had ever hoped for...

Jackie came up quietly and for once did not start talking. Instead she just put her arm around her only daughter.

'He's gone,' sobbed Rose. 'He's left me, Mum. He's left me.'

She sobbed even harder, and Jackie, who knew a thing or two about unreliable men, kissed her forehead and stroked her shoulder and crooned, 'It's all right, it's all right, I'm sorry...'

She was still murmuring her sympathy as all the windows in the flat smashed, as every window on the estate shattered, and as the glass-showered earth beneath their feet began to tremble and things came crashing to the ground.

Every window in London smashed, and still it did not jolt the frozen sleepers, standing up at the very heights, as broken glass rained down on their terrified loved ones gathered below.

Groaning heavily, a huge rock moved into the sky, casting its shadow over everything; the massive belly-shaking rumble of the noise it made felt across the city. Its darkness seemed all the more awful in the bright white winter's morning of Christmas Day.

Llewelyn was screaming at the screen, as the alarms came on, shouting that it was the sonic wave of the spaceship hitting the atmosphere, but everywhere else nobody had a clue.

He was right, for all that it mattered: the ship hit the atmosphere, and the shockwave reverberated around the world.

'Here it comes,' he said, clinging on to the back of his chair, as if that could save him.

None of the people standing on the edges looked up. But their loved ones did, and the screams and panic were terrible to hear. Their imprecations grew stronger, the more they attempted to pull people away. In Calais, a man, trying to save his wife, lost his footing on a warehouse roof, and tumbled to his own doom. His wife did not give him a second glance as he fell.

The great ship looming over London could be seen for a hundred miles. It was like a huge grey boulder; somehow hanging there in mid air, both organic and engineered at the same time.

Then the screaming fell silent. *Everything* fell silent.

In a different time, Rose would have stood. She would have fought. She would have been in the centre of any battle, with the Doctor at her side.

Now all of that had been ended. She had no strategy; she had no plan. She had the two people in the world she was closest to, and that was going to have to do.

She dashed indoors, pulled the sheets off the Doctor.

'Mickey, we're going to carry him. Mum, get your stuff, and get some food. We're going.'

Mickey shrugged.

'Where to?'

Rose glanced up.

'The TARDIS. It's the only safe place on Earth.'

'What we going to do in there?' asked Jackie, bemused.

Rose looked up, utterly defeated.

'Hide,' she said softly.

'Is that it?' said Jackie.

'Mum! Look in the sky. There's a great big alien invasion, and I don't know what to do, all right? I've travelled with him, and I've seen all that stuff, but when I'm stuck at home I'm useless. Now all we can do is run and hide, and I'm sorry. Now move.'

Jackie vanished to do as she was told. Rose heaved the Doctor up, taking the shoulder end; Mickey took the legs.

'Right! Lift!'

Harriet Jones stared hard at the huge screen. The sinister bone-faced aliens were back, gathered once more in formation.

'They're transmitting,' warned Llewellyn, every muscle tensed.

Alex ran the harsh, guttural speech through his handheld computer, and translated for them: '"*You are now our property*"—well, that's more like "goods and chattels". Um. "*Now will the tribal leader*"—that's just "leader" I suppose—*"will the leader of this world stand forward."*

Harriet Jones immediately did so. Her face was composed.

'I'm proud to represent this planet.'

'*SOO CAL FORAXI!*' screamed the Leader on screen.

'That means... um...' Alex looked up, his eyes frightened. '"*Come aboard.*"'

'Well, how do I do that?' said Harriet Jones, but just as she did so, all four of them were bathed in the blue light—they looked around at each other, eyes frightened.

'Wh- What's happening?' cried Llewellyn.

'I would imagine it's called a teleport,' said Harriet Jones. 'Or a transmat. One of those words—'And she was still talking as they vanished into the ether, leaving the remaining UNIT staff staring aghast into empty space.

Daniel Llewellyn's first thought upon arriving on the spaceship was that it didn't look like a spaceship at all.

It was more like a dark Gothic amphitheatre. Much of it was in darkness, and torches burned on the wall. Huge torn red banners were hung along the sides, and the vast space was lined with benches. Row upon row of aliens sat upon them, tightly packed, staring down at the vast stage that their visitors from Earth now stood upon.

The astonishing speed of the teleportation had messed with Llewellyn's head, but not before he'd seen quite clearly in front of him thousands and thousands more of the menacing alien faces that had appeared on screen. The creatures were absolutely as huge and dangerous-looking as he'd feared, and the great room smelled of something hot and menacing: bodies, ready for battle. A fair distance away, across the metal floor, was the formation of Sycorax aliens they had seen on the monitor.

One, slightly taller than the rest, and dressed in what appeared to be decorated battle armour—the one they'd seen on the screen—stepped forward. The four humans instinctively did the same. Then a surprising thing happened: the Sycorax Leader lifted his hand to his horrifying skull-like face.

'That's a helmet!' cried Llewellyn with sudden hope. 'This thing—it might be like us!' For a moment, that hope surged as he imagined the face of some sheepish, smirking human being beneath the mask— that all of this was some elaborate, incredible stunt, a monumental prank. Why or how anyone could have done such a thing, he could not imagine—he knew only that there might be hope.

Slowly the alien removed the hideous carapace— to reveal an even more menacing alien face of raw flesh and tight bone and sharp pointed teeth underneath.

'Or not,' finished Llewellyn softly, as the alien started to bark at them in his strange, fierce language.

'*PADSKAA!*' screeched the Sycorax Leader. The humans stared at Alex, who was gazing around with his mouth hanging open.

'Padskaa?' prompted Harriet.

Alex shook his head. 'Sorry. Um. "*Welcome.*"'

'*KA, JALVAAAN.*'

Alex looked up, awkwardly.

'"*Now, surrender.*"'

'*JALVAAN! JALVAAN!*' screamed the Sycorax Leader, and in the huge gallery around them, the Sycorax took up the chant; rattling their bone jewellery; banging staffs against the ground and waving their broadswords; all of one voice: *JALVAAN! JALVAAN! JALVAAN!*

The sound of the aliens' screams shook the foundations of the blood-red cavern. The four humans standing in place felt small and helpless and terribly, terribly alone.

14

Stop the Cavalry

Rose and Mickey were struggling to manoeuvre the Doctor out of the flat's front door, one at each end—Mickey had the feet, Rose had her arms under the stranger's shoulders, his head pressed up against her stomach. Jackie had several shopping bags and kept dropping them. All around them was pandemonium: people rushing to and fro, or tending the wounded who'd caught the worst of the shattered glass, or simply gazing up at the dark shadow of the ship. Still, on the rooftops, the sinister lines of people waited, watched; statues on ledges; carved gargoyles and angels.

'Mum, will you just leave that stuff and give us a hand?' shouted Rose.

'It's food!' said Jackie. She was already bamboozled. She'd only been inside the box a couple of times, but she knew it was somehow huge. They must have a kitchen. They travelled the universe, didn't they? She knew her Rose wasn't eating properly when she was away, she was far too thin. *His* fault, again, this Doctor, or this stranger who—

'Just leave it!' shouted Rose.

Jackie thought that if there was a kitchen after all it would have been useful to know before. And if everything was as bad as Rose said, they might be in there a while...

In a tizz, she dumped some of the bags and trailed along after the short procession. If things were going to get bad, she thought, they'd still want a sandwich.

Back on the Sycorax ship, Alex was still translating. The aggressive tone of the Sycorax Leader was not, as he'd hoped, a linguistic twitch. It was simply aggression. The fact that Alex himself had a soft, refined voice made the terrible threats sound almost worse.

The Sycorax Leader stood behind a huge dais made of black twisted metal. His scaly hand hovered over a huge red switch on the top. All of them stared at it. It was obvious what it must be, even before Alex could say the words.

'*"You will surrender, or I will release the final curse. And your people will jump."*'

Llewellyn's heart sank. He had never been a brave man; or rather, he had never, in all his universities and labs, been tested. He had never known. And in his careless, boundless optimism at what might be out beyond the stars, he had directly threatened the lives of a third of all the humans on Earth.

His thoughts sprang back to Sally Jacobs suddenly, and a hot drink on cold steps, and winter sunlight on golden hair. He thought of the lines of people around the world, on the highest cliffs, that would haunt his dreams forever.

He had no choice. He pushed his way to the front of the group, swallowed back the urge to be sick.

'If… if I can speak…?'

The Major attempted to pull him back. 'Mr Llewellyn! You're a civilian—'

Daniel shook his head. His mind was made up.

'No. I sent out this probe. I started it. It made contact with these people; this whole thing's my responsibility.'

He pulled his arm out of Blake's grasp and stepped forward.

The Sycorax Leader turned to face him.

Llewellyn had never felt more frightened than when the great red eyes sought him out; nor more sure that what he was doing was the right thing.

'With respect… Sir. I created the probe—the *Guinevere One*. I wanted to reach out in friendship. The human race is taking its first step towards the stars. But we are like children compared to you. Children who need help. Children who need compassion. I beg of you now—show that compassion.'

Just for a moment, there was a hope. For a tiny split second, the entire room fell silent, waiting to see what would happen. Llewellyn realised his heart was beating incredibly fast; he could feel the blood rushing in his ears. But to meet an advanced people with reason, with language. It was an encounter he'd dreamed would happen his entire life. And if he could save Sally from that windswept ledge far below, now… save them all…

The Sycorax Leader gazed at Llewellyn. Its pointed tongue hung outside its mouth. Its face slowly twisted in, what—respect, understanding?

Amusement?

It happened so fast: the alien, raised, suddenly, a whip from his side, and lashed it out with a sharp electrical crack of blue light. It fastened around Daniel Llewellyn's neck, burning and tightening at the same time.

Llewellyn let out a scream which faded to nothing. His body shuddered and then every dream he'd ever had; every plan he had ever made, every thought he'd ever entertained, every step on the path of the life he'd led was no more. Every cell of him flew on the wind, as the good man he'd been exploded into a pile of smoking bones scattering over the floor.

Immediately the Major leapt forward while Harriet Jones tried to stay calm, her brown eyes looking at the situation levelly; weighing up her options. Fixing in her mind the face of the young man who had sacrificed himself for principles of peace.

Meanwhile Major Blake was shouting. 'That man was your prisoner! Even your species must have articles of war, forbidding—'

Harriet saw the whip hand lifting. There was a terrible, terrible scent in the air: of blood and burning bones and everything dreadful.

She moved forwards. She remembered her first week as Prime Minister—a blur of photocalls and protocol and official cars and new information—and the first time she had descended into the UNIT facility. He had been so gracious; not condescending, like many of the civil servants she had met, or patronising, like the military generals who assumed she wouldn't have a clue what she was talking about. He had shaken her hand firmly, given a short smile and said, 'I believe you have some experience in these areas, and that's likely to be a very great asset.' Harriet had found herself unexpectedly grateful; she had liked him very much.

And the great, bony hand with its long pointed fingers was wielding the whip once again, and Harriet gasped aloud in shock; made to step forward to stop this creature somehow. But it was too late. There was no time even to beg.

The alien slaughtered the Major in front of her eyes, and the smell got worse and Harriet could feel the blood ringing in her ears as she thought to herself, 'This is it. This is it.'

She forced herself forward and tried to steady her voice. 'Harriet Jones,' she announced, 'Prime Minister.'

Alex, his voice an exhausted monotone now, had to translate the howls and grunts of the Sycorax Leader: '*TASS CONAFEE TEDRO SOO!*'

'"*Yes, we know who you are,*"' Alex said. '"*Surrender or they will die.*"'

The Leader held his hand over the red switch again.

'If I do surrender,' said Harriet calmly, 'how would that be better?'

The great bony pointed hand was now almost on top of the red button as he replied, and Harriet could barely hear Alex's translation above the rumbling approval of those Sycorax watching.

'"*We will summon the Armada and take only half of your population. The rest you can keep. One-half is sold into slavery or one-third dies.*"'

The creature smiled a terrible smile.

'*SOO CODSYLA.*'

'"*Your choice,*"' said Alex, his voice a whisper.

Harriet Jones closed her eyes. The leader of the Sycorax hissed. The rest of the chamber fell silent.

Jackie Tyler looked around the console room, trying to take it all in. A sofa would have been nice, she thought. But at least they had a telly.

'No chance you can fly this thing?' said Mickey to Rose. He was good with technical challenges, but didn't have a clue where to start with this.

'Not any more, no,' said Rose. Being here without the Doctor—without her Doctor, even as they held another man's body in their arms—was opening up a huge emptiness in her heart. The entire TARDIS, normally such a living entity to her, suddenly felt cold and dead as the grave.

'Well, you did it before,' said Mickey.

'I know.' Rose glanced away. She knew that looking into the heart of the TARDIS was out. 'It's sort of been… wiped out of my head, like it's forbidden. Try it again and I think the universe rips in half.'

'Ah, better not, then.'

'Maybe not.'

They carefully placed the Doctor on the floor. Rose realised she'd been hoping that as soon as they walked in, everything would light up; come to life; go back to how it was. But he remained a statue; a fallen knight in a dressing gown, now inside his unlikely tomb.

Mickey looked around helplessly. 'So, what do we do? Just sit here?'

Rose was so frustrated she could cry. All this power, all this glory in this box and absolutely nothing anyone could do, even when everyone was looking to her.

'That's as good as it gets,' she said.

Jackie took out her flask. 'Right. Here we go. Nice cup of tea.'

'Oh, the solution to everything,' said Rose, ungratefully.

'Now, stop your moaning. I'll get the rest of the food.'

She bustled out of the TARDIS, as Rose leaned against the console, staring at the Doctor. Mickey shook his head as he picked up the thermos.

'Tea. Like we're having a picnic while the world comes to an end. Very British. Chin-chin.'

Rose wasn't listening. Mickey fiddled with the scanner on the console.

'How does this thing work? It picks up TV, maybe we could see what's going on out there. Maybe we've surrendered?' He pushed a few random buttons. 'What do you do to it?'

'I don't know... it sort of tunes itself.'

Realising he was only trying to help, she too pressed a few buttons...

And on the war deck of the Sycorax spaceship, the Leader felt each press of those buttons—felt the ripples in the universe—and stared round at his people, his red face more furious than ever. '*SOO HEB CLSHVORDAL CASYBID!!!!!*'

The vast roomful of Sycorax started to screech and beat their staves to the ground. The Leader pointed at Harriet, who looked helplessly at Alex.

'The noise, the bleeping, they say it's machinery. *"Foreign machinery."* They're accusing us of hiding it. Conspiring.' He glanced up, his young face haggard with fear, as the Sycorax Leader gestured to one of the other aliens.

'CREL STAT FORAXI!'

Alex translated for Harriet: *"'Bring it on board.'"*

Jackie Tyler thought she might as well bring the rest of the bags, which had Christmas dinner in them. Save it going to waste, she decided. The world wasn't going to end in the next twenty seconds, was it? No. They had tea and they'd have turkey and in a bit, hopefully, this would all be sorted out...

She had nearly made it back to the blue box when it dematerialised. She stared upwards; but all she could see was the dark vastness of the Sycorax ship, blotting out the sun, and Jackie screamed the name of her only child to the frozen air.

15

A Spaceman Came Travelling

The TARDIS scanner hadn't turned itself on, but it was beeping.

'What's that?' Mickey looked uneasy. 'Maybe it's a distress signal.'

'Fat lot of good that's going to do,' said Rose.

'Are you going to be this much of a misery all the time?'

'Yes,' said Rose.

Mickey sighed and tried to lighten the mood. 'You should look at it from my point of view, stuck in here with your mum's cooking.'

Rose glanced around. 'Where is she?' It struck her suddenly that she shouldn't have let her mother leave, and she jumped to her feet. 'I'd better go and give her a hand; it might start raining missiles out there.'

Mickey smiled. 'Tell her anything from a tin is fine.'

'Why don't you tell her yourself?'

'I'm not that brave,' said Mickey.

Rose looked at her old boyfriend, this decent man she knew had lost so many of his own hopes and dreams. 'Oh, I don't know,' she said softly, and opened the door, as Mickey smiled back at her.

Then Rose was grabbed around the arm by a huge, horned hand, and screamed.

'Rose!' Mickey leapt up, knocking over the flask of tea onto the grille by the Doctor's head.

Rose was screaming, 'GET OFF! GET OFF ME!'

Without hesitation, Mickey ran after her. Bathed in blood-red light, skin prickling in sudden, swampy heat, he realised the police box had moved. Now he stood in the vast chamber of an alien ship, surrounded by the monsters he'd seen on television.

And now Rose was screaming at him. 'Close the door! Close the door!'

Just in time he wheeled back and pulled the TARDIS door closed.

Rose was struggling in the grip of an alien. Another grabbed Mickey's shoulders before he could take a second step, as the Leader screeched a war cry of glee, and the onlookers cheered and stamped their feet in triumph.

Inside the TARDIS the tea began to drip, drip drip onto the console room lights, and the hot lights started to steam.

As the steam rose, the Doctor's mouth opened. He took a deep breath, and when he released it, his thin lips sparkled as the gold energy streamed from his mouth.

'*GLASSHEEVEN,*' barked the Sycorax Leader, and the humans were roughly herded together.

Harriet saw her first. *Rose!*

Rose was here! And if Rose was here... *he* must be here too...

Relief cascaded through Harriet like a waterfall and she was close to tears as she pulled Rose into her arms and hugged her tight. 'I've got you! I've got you! Oh my Lord, you precious thing.'

She held her close, whispering, 'Where's the Doctor? is he with you?'

'No,' Rose whispered shakily. 'We're all on our own.'

Inside Harriet, the waterfall froze, in a second, to solid ice.

The Sycorax army regarded her balefully.

Inside the TARDIS, with aching slowness, the very last of the tea fell onto the hot lights; the very last of the steam coiled upwards; the very last drops lingering over the Doctor.

The Sycorax Leader was even more terrifying up close. He pointed straight at Rose and screamed at her. Alex stumbled forward to translate.

'"*The yellow girl. She has the clever blue box. Therefore she speaks for your planet.*"'

'But she can't!!' said Harriet in anguish.

Rose hadn't taken her eyes off the Leader. She knew there was no one else who could do this; who'd seen the things she'd seen.

She wasn't the Doctor. But she was the closest thing the Earth was going to get.

'Yeah, I *can* do this,' she whispered.

'Don't you dare,' said Mickey.

'Somebody's got to be the Doctor.'

Harriet grabbed her arm, terrified. 'They'll kill you.'

'Never stopped him.'

Rose took more steps towards the Sycorax Leader. There was excitement in the air now; the watching hordes were muttering excitedly. Now she could see more clearly, Rose noted just how many there were. She swallowed.

Well, here goes nothing.

Rose cleared her throat, a tiny sound in the silent amphitheatre. 'I, um… I address the Sycorax according to… Article 15 of the Shadow Proclamation.' Her voice was shaking. 'I command you to leave this world with all the authority of the Slitheen Parliament of Raxacoricofallapatorius, and um… the Gelth Confederacy…'

The Sycorax leader stared at her, fascinated, but Rose continued defiantly. 'As, uh… sanctioned… by the

Mighty Jagrafess… and… Oh, the Daleks! Now, leave this planet in peace! In peace…'

The Leader couldn't take his eyes off her. There were a few seconds of stunned silence, and then, slowly, he grunted and started to shake. The others did the same. And then it became clear: they were laughing. The entire citadel of Sycorax laughed; roared, hooted like animals.

Rose's heart plunged. They knew. Of course they knew how ridiculous she as was being, how powerless she was.

'*SOO GAN, GAN PRACTEEL.*'

Loyal Alex stood, trembling. '"*You are very, very funny.*"'

'*SOO GAL CHACK CHIFF.*'

'"*And now you are going to die.*"'

The Sycorax Leader took his whip in his hand.

Harriet and Mickey lunged forward at the same time. 'Leave her alone!' Harriet shouted.

'Don't touch her!' Mickey's voice cracked as he started forward, but like Harriet he had been seized by the huge, hideous guards, as the Sycorax Leader kept his attention on Rose, circling her slowly. She stood like a statue, pale as ice.

'*SOO TASS GILFANE?*'

'"*Did you think you were clever?*"' Alex translated, dully.

'*MET SOO VOL STAPEEN?*'

'"*With your stolen words?*"'

123

'*CODRAFEE PEL VASH...*'

"*We have travelled in the wastelands...*"

'*CODRAFEE NON PASSIC PEL·HADAR TOC TANE BRENDISSA!*'

"*We care nothing for your*"—uhm— "*tiny legislation of land-bound species!*"

'*CODRAFEE SYCORA!*'

"*We are Sycorax.*"

'*CODRAFEE GASSAC TEL DASHFELLIK!*'

"*We bestride the darkness.*"

Mickey was not listening, just staring, helpless. Desperate. 'Please don't hurt Rose. Please...'

But the leader stepped closer; enjoying every moment of Rose's fear; flexing his whip. She took a step backwards; back towards the safety of the TARDIS now denied her. He went on; inexorably continued. Alex's kept his eyes on the translator; even as he had to bear witness; was compelled to speak.

'*CORAFEE PEL SAT COS JISAAAN. ORD STOLTO GAVI CONASTROFAAA.*'

"*We practise the forbidden arts. The lost rites of Astrophia.*"

'*BEC CODRAKONE, SOO FEL NAS CHAFEEN.*'

"*Next to us, you are but a wailing child.*"

'*IF SO FALFASS YOUR PLANET CASTREEK AS CHAMPION!*'

"*If you are the best your planet can offer as a champion.*"

'*THEN YOUR WORLD WILL BE GUTTED, FEL YOUR PEOPLE ENSLAVED.*'

124

'"Then your world will be gutted, and your people ensla— "Hold on.' Alex was staring at his screen like it had just exploded. 'That's English.'

The humans stared at each other in consternation, all except for Rose, of course.

Rose knew.

She pointed at the Sycorax Leader in barely contained glee. 'You're talking English!'

'I WOULD NEVER DIRTY MY TONGUE WITH YOUR PRIMITIVE BILE!'

'But that's English!' Rose continued to back, subtly, towards the TARDIS. 'Can you hear English?' she shouted to the others.

'That's English!' agreed Mickey delighted.

Harriet nodded. 'Definitely English,' said Alex.

The Sycorax Leader was incensed. 'I SPEAK ONLY SYCORAXIC!'

'But if I can hear English...' said Rose, steeling herself to dare to speak aloud the news she could barely believe, 'then it's being translated. Which means the TARDIS is working. Which means...'

And she turned around slowly, trembling; hardly daring to hope.

Mickey and Harriet turned around too. And suddenly, the TARDIS doors swung open to reveal a figure—no, *not* a figure, Rose realised, finally. Not another person; not a man, not a succubus, or an apparition. For the first time she believed it inside, heart and soul.

The Doctor.

The Doctor was there, standing in the TARDIS doorway, still wearing those ridiculous pyjamas, a vast, slightly unhinged grin plastered across his face.

'Did you miss me?' he said loudly.

16

I Wonder as I Wander

Missed you? thought Rose. *Right down to my bones*. And she grinned with utter delight, even in the perilous situation they were in, surrounded by the enemy, five miles above the Earth.

The Doctor stepped forward, the TARDIS doors slamming shut behind him.

The Sycorax Leader immediately roared in fury and lashed out his whip at the Doctor who, without missing a beat, grabbed the end. It had absolutely no effect on him. He tore it out of the leader's hand.

'Careful,' he said. 'You could have someone's eye out with that.'

The Sycorax Leader roared once more and ran at the Doctor with his huge wooden staff, but the Doctor grabbed it and snapped it over his knee like it was a matchstick. 'You just can't get the staff,' he said, and Rose winced, as she always did when the Doctor told one of his terrible jokes.

'Now, *you*…' The Doctor extended a long finger and pointed it ominously at the Sycorax Leader. 'You wait. I'm busy.'

Such was the authority in the Doctor's voice that the Sycorax leader did as he was told. The Sycorax holding the others stepped back too, uncertain, biding their time as the Doctor roamed the huge floorspace as if perfectly happy to be there. Rose stared at him, amazed.

'Nice place,' he said. 'Roomy. Bit dark. Must cost a fortune, heating this place.'

He approached the others.

'Mickey! Hello! And Harriet Jones, MP for Flydale North! Blimey, it's like *This Is Your Life*!'

He turned to Rose, who had an eyebrow raised.

'Tea!' he proclaimed. 'That's all I needed. A good cup of tea! A superheated infusion of free radicals and tannin. Just the thing for healing the synapses, whose idea was that, a cup of tea?'

'That was my mother,' said Rose.

'And why can I taste shampoo?'

'That… was also my mother.'

'Could be worse, she could be here.' With a glance round at the Sycorax to be sure they were still behaving, the Doctor went up to her and lowered his voice.

'First things first. Now, be honest this time. How do I look?'

'Um. Different,' said Rose.

'Good different or bad different?'

Rose was absolutely not going to get into this conversation right now. She didn't want to discuss how different. How much younger. How much…

'Just… different,' she said.

'Am I ginger?'

Rose glanced at him to see if he was serious. He appeared to be. 'No, you're just kind of brown.'

'Aww, I wanted to be ginger. I've never been ginger.'

His mood changed suddenly, and he pointed straight at her.

'And you, Rose Tyler, fat lot of good you were, you gave up on me.' He stopped suddenly. 'Oh, that's rude. Is that the sort of man I am now, am I? Rude.' He pondered this a little further. 'Rude and not ginger.'

Harriet interjected. 'I'm sorry, but who is this?'

'I'm the Doctor.'

'He's the Doctor,' said Rose, tentatively.

'He is, he's the Doctor,' added Mickey with just a hint of resignation.

'But what happened to *my* Doctor?' said Harriet, bemused. 'Is it a title that's just passed on?'

The Doctor walked towards her, right up close to her face. 'I'm him. I'm literally him. Same man, new face, well… New everything.'

Harriet looked more confused than ever.

'But you can't be.'

He didn't take his eyes off her. 'Harriet Jones. We were trapped in Downing Street, and the one thing that scared you wasn't the aliens… wasn't the war… it was the thought of your mother being on her own.'

Harriet blinked several times. 'Oh my God.'

'Did you win the election?' The Doctor beamed.

Harriet smiled back, pleased. 'Landslide majority.'

'Oh, fantast—no. Hold on. Fantas. Fanta. Fantazz.' He wandered off. 'Can't say it any more, doesn't fit the teeth. Ohh, I liked that word, what am I going to say now? "Brilliant"? Brilliant, brill-ee-ant, briiiiilliant. No. Um. "Excellent"? "Oh, that's excellent!" Naaa. "Superb!"? "Marvellous!" *Molto bene!* Oh, I don't know. Let's just settle for "very, very good". "That's very, very good. Yes that's really very, very good." Not taking off, is it?'

The roar came from behind them. 'IF I MIGHT INTERRUPT?' roared the Sycorax Leader.

The Doctor spun around. 'Yes! Sorry! Hello, big fella!' He could see the trepidation of the unknown in the creature's eyes was giving way to a cold, face-saving rage.

'WHO EXACTLY ARE YOU?'

'Well,' said the Doctor, grinning. 'That's the question. Nice ship, by the way, sturdy, good gravity, kind of rocky—'

'I DEMAND TO KNOW WHO YOU ARE!'

'*I don't know!*' the Doctor roared back, and Rose looked at him; recognised something else besides that dangerous smile: anger. The same anger the Doctor always denied he even felt.

The Doctor carried on.

'See, there's the thing. I'm the Doctor, but beyond that, I… I just don't know. I literally do not know who I am. It's all untested. Am I funny? Am I sarcastic?' He winked at Rose. 'Sexy?'

Rose bit her lip and grinned nervously, really wishing he hadn't looked at her when he'd said that, but he was barrelling onwards.

'A right old misery? Life and soul? Right-handed? Left-handed? A gambler? A fighter? A coward? A traitor? A liar? A nervous wreck? I mean, judging by the evidence, I've certainly got a gob.' Suddenly, he caught sight of the red switch on top of the dais. His face lit up. 'And how am I going to react when I see this? A great big threatening button?'

He ran towards it, and Rose was both reassured and concerned to notice that he was laughing.

'A Great Big Threatening Button Which Must Not Be Pressed Under Any Circumstances—am I right? Let me guess, it's some sort of control matrix? Hmm? Hold on, what's feeding it?' The Doctor bent down and pulled open a small cupboard beneath the button. Inside was a tank bubbling with thick red liquid. 'And what've we got here? Blood?'

Rose knew he was going to taste it before he did so. Oh God, how could she ever have doubted he was the same, infuriating, unpredictable Doctor.

'Yeah. Definitely. Blood. Human Blood. A positive. Now I can taste blood *and* shampoo. Bleargh. But if you've got a matrix dipped into that…' He made a face as if he found it disgusting, which was, Rose supposed, a blessing of sorts, and wiped his dirty finger on his dressing gown. Then he slapped his own head. 'Ahh! But that means… blood control. Blood control! Oh, I haven't seen blood control for years! You're controlling all the A positives!'

Rose wasn't sure, but she thought the Sycorax Leader looked slightly deflated. The Doctor looked more energised than ever.

'Which leaves us with a great big stinking problem. 'Cos I really don't know who I am. I don't know when to stop. So if I see a Great Big Threatening Button Which Should Never Ever EVER Be Pressed… then I just wanna do *this*.'

And before anyone had the chance to stop him, he banged his hand down hard on the button.

17

Ding Dong! Merrily on High

Everyone on top of the walls, all over the world, took one step forward. Until they were on the very tips of their feet, right on the edge, and the two-thirds of the world held its breath, or screamed, or panicked; or, like Matthew Nicholson, who had finally found a lift to take him to the roof, found himself with his arms hooked around his friend Duerte in such a precarious way that meant that if one fell, they were both going over.

And the A positives raised their feet to take the final, crucial steps—whereupon the blue webs of light blinked—wavered—

And disappeared.

There was a great collective stomp of flesh and leather on concrete as the zombies awoke and took sudden, staggering steps back from the edge. Duerte fell, extremely confused, into Matthew's lap, and two went rolling backwards, Matthew yelling with joy.

*

At the Powell Estate, Sandra screamed for the hundredth time at her boyfriend Jason, 'GET AWAY FROM THE EDGE!'

It was not just Jason, but half the estate up there that heard her—and they took it as an instant instruction; and turned round, shook themselves, confused, as if they didn't know where they were.

'What the bloody hell am I doing up here?' grumbled Jason. 'How much did I have to drink last night?'

At the Tower of London a blonde girl stared over the city, and blinked. Then she turned around. Everywhere, people were being greeted by tearful friends and partners; hugging them; holding them; desperately pleased to see them again.

There was nobody there for her.

She turned around; freezing cold, her mind baffled—why had she been so convinced all she wanted to do was stand on a roof? What had happened? She had had specialist training against this kind of thing, and it hadn't worked at all.

And then she glanced upwards and realised immediately, seeing the huge dark outline of the ship, that their problems weren't over, not by a long shot, and she headed back into the Tower to work.

She wondered if that nice Welsh bloke was downstairs and if he might fancy another cup of coffee...

*

Up in the ship, everyone was still staring in horror at the button the Doctor had pressed.

'You killed them!' shouted Alex.

'Oh shut up! Don't be so stupid,' said the Doctor. Then he stopped himself. 'Blimey, this rudeness thing is out of control. Sorry!'

He turned to the Sycorax Leader.

'What do you think, Big Fella? Are they dead?'

The Sycorax Leader, for once, seemed thrown. 'We… allow them to live.'

'Allow? You've no choice!' crowed the Doctor. He turned back to the baffled humans. 'I mean, that's all blood control is—a cheap bit of voodoo. Scares the pants off you, but that's as far as it goes. It's like hypnosis—you can hypnotise someone to walk like a chicken or sing like Elvis, but you can't hypnotise them to death. Survival instinct's too strong.'

The Sycorax Leader turned round and hissed. 'Blood control was merely one form of conquest. I can summon the Armada and take this world by force.'

The Doctor was toying with him now. 'Well, yeah, you *could*, yeah, you *could* do that, of course you could. But why? Look at these people. These human beings. Consider their potential. From the day they arrive on the planet and blinking step into the sun. There is more to see than can ever be seen. More to do than… No, hold on…' He stared to the side for a moment.

'Sorry, that's *The Lion King*. But the point still stands. Leave them alone!'

'Or what?' said the Sycorax Leader.

The Doctor glanced around. 'Or...' Suddenly, he grabbed a sword straight from a stone container. He charged down the steps and stood in front of the TARDIS, then he raised the sword high into the air like a warrior.

'I challenge you!' he shouted.

Rose, staring aghast, wasn't at all expecting what came next: a huge roar of approval from the Sycorax, which echoed throughout the amphitheatre. The Doctor, however, was completely unperturbed.

'Oh, now that's struck a chord,' he said. 'Am I right— the sanctified rules of combat still apply?'

The Sycorax Leader slowly descended the steps, unsheathing his huge sword. He was much, much bigger than the Doctor. 'You stand as this world's champion?'

The Doctor thought for a moment. 'Thank you.' He took off his dressing gown and threw it to Rose, who caught it easily. 'I don't know who I am—but you just summed me up.'

He raised his sword.

'So. You accept my challenge? Or are you just a *krallak pelle dalla sheestok*?'

The audience rose to its feet, howling and chanting. The Leader looked around.

'For the planet?' he growled.

The Doctor grinned and nodded. 'For the planet!'

With a bloodcurdling scream, the Sycorax Leader swung his broadsword.

The Doctor blocked the Sycorax Leader's sword stroke with his own blade. Sparks flew as the huge, heavy old instruments of war sung together.

The leader launched himself at the Doctor, his blade swinging as the Doctor parried. There was no grace or finesse to the way they fought with the broadswords; nothing like Rose had seen on films. It was raw, clunking and loud, the huge weight of the heavy broadswords clanging on the raw metal of the spaceship floor. The Doctor lost the first skirmish, driven back towards the TARDIS doors.

The Sycorax were yelling and screaming as if they were at a sports match, which perhaps they were; the humans cowered into themselves, hypnotised by the fight. Rose thought she'd be horrified. But she found she was also excited as the Doctor and the Sycorax Leader circled each other, wielding their huge weapons in fury.

Suddenly the Doctor was besting the Sycorax leader, bearing down on him, pushing him back with stroke after bone-ringing stroke. His teeth were gritted. 'Thing is, I still don't know who I am. Am I fighter? Am I a swordsman? Am I an expert? Am I the sort of man who could happily slaughter you, have you thought of that?'

He was on top of the Sycorax Leader now.

'What if I'm a killer?'

In a tremendous push, the Sycorax Leader hurled him off, and fought back in a flurry of blows; and now it was the Doctor on the back foot, taking a pummelling.

CRACK! went the swords in the air

'What if I'm not?'

CRACK! and his arm was forced down again

'Actually I don't think I am.'

KKLAK!

'Definitely not a killer, no. Which, if you a think about it, is a good thing.' The Doctor tripped over his own feet, stumbled over backwards. 'Ah. But not right now…'

The Sycorax Leader swung his sword. Swift as lightning the Doctor rolled out of the way as the blow came down, missing him by inches.

'Look out!' Rose couldn't stop herself from screaming.

'Oh yeah, that helped,' the Doctor yelled. 'Wouldn't have thought of that otherwise, thanks.'

The Sycorax Leader hadn't stopped pressing his advantage, forcing the Doctor back once more against the dripping, rocky edge of the amphitheatre. The Doctor was obviously weakening; his legs looked ready to fold like those of a new-born fawn, and there was nowhere else to run. He glanced behind him at the wall—and then he saw it.

'Bit of fresh air?' said the Doctor. And he slammed his fist on the large wall button, which immediately opening a sliding door—leading out into the open air, onto the great, sprawling wing of the vast ship.

The sky was blazing blue around them; the wind cut like cheese-wire, the air thin and freezing. London was plainly visible, far far below, and all of the humans, and some of the Sycorax, ventured out to watch the fight play out. There was, Rose noticed with alarm, no barrier around the open space at all; nothing to stop them all plummeting miles to their deaths. She tore her gaze away from the Doctor long enough to glimpse the familiar landmarks below, then quickly stopped as her stomach twisted. It twisted again as she saw the Sycorax Leader still had the upper hand; she started forward but the Doctor immediately held up an arm to stop her.

'Stay back!' he snarled. 'Invalidate the challenge and he wins the planet!' The Sycorax Leader landed a blow that nearly knocked the sword from the Doctor's grip. 'Oh, you're just *nasty*. You know, I'm not even wearing slippers!'

The Doctor rallied once again. The two warriors were so different, but both were furiously wrestling for control, grimacing at one another.

Finally, with a bellow, the Sycorax Leader simply shoved the Doctor away with all his might. The Doctor staggered back, out of control, fell flat on his back at the very edge of the spaceship's wing.

The Sycorax Leader raised his blade and sliced down with horrible force—cutting straight through the Doctor's sword arm, severing it at the wrist. The Doctor watched in utter disbelief as his hand, the sword still clutched in dead fingers, skittered over the side of the ship and fell towards the Earth below.

18

Happy Xmas (War is Over)

The Sycorax Leader started laughing. Mickey and Alex had looked away, unable to watch any longer.

Rose burst into shocked tears, but couldn't turn her back on the Doctor.

The Doctor stared at the space where his arm had been; the empty sleeve. 'You cut my hand off!'

The Sycorax Leader let out a horrible toothy grin of triumph. 'Yah! SYCORAX!' he snarled, raising his sword high.

Then there was no sound but the wind on the floating platform. There was, Rose noticed, no blood. She had always wondered. If he bled.

The Doctor got to his feet. His face, strangely, was triumphant.

'And now,' he said. 'Now, I know what sort of man I am.'

The others stared at him.

'I'm lucky. 'Cos quite by chance … I'm still within the first fifteen hours of my regeneration cycle. Which means I've got just enough residual cellular energy… to do this…'

And he held up his empty sleeve. And in front of everyone's eyes, a glowing, golden cloud of matter, of raw regeneration energy, filled the space where his hand had been. Pink, quivering flesh quested out through the sleeve and started to turn, quite clearly, into a hand. A brand new hand, flexing, alive.

'WITCHCRAFT!' shrieked the Sycorax Leader.

'Time Lord,' the Doctor corrected him.

Without wasting a second, Rose grabbed another sword off the nearest Sycorax.

And for the first time since he woke up, she called him by his name. '*Doctor!*'

The Doctor caught it by the hilt with his brand new hand and turned to face her. 'So, I'm still the Doctor, then?'

Rose grinned. 'No arguments from me.'

The Doctor smiled back because, of course, he knew that there were always going to be arguments from Rose Tyler.

He turned back to the Sycorax Leader. 'Want to know the best bit? This new hand…' He put on a cowboy voice, just to see if he could do one, which he could, just about. 'It's a *fighting hand*!'

And gleefully, brilliantly, he ran hard at the Sycorax Leader and the fight began once more with a new and incredible energy, the sound of the swords clanging like an alarm, the Leader now defensive, the Doctor utterly unstoppable; thrusting the hilt of his sword into the Leader's stomach so that the creature doubled over, even as the watching humans winced.

With one final massive swing from the Doctor, the Sycorax Leader's sword went flying from his hand, slithering across the wing deck like a rat fleeing light. The Leader fell onto his back, panting for breath, dangerously close to the edge and the dizzying drop beyond.

The Doctor stood over him, breathing heavily. He pointed his sword at the Sycorax Leader's throat. 'I win,' he said simply.

'Then kill me,' said the Sycorax Leader, still defiant.

The Doctor blinked. 'I'll spare your life if you'll take this champion's command: leave this planet and never return. What do you say?'

'Yes,' croaked the Sycorax Leader immediately.

The Doctor leaned in low; quiet and deadly. 'Swear on the blood of your species.'

'I swear,' said the Sycorax.

There was a pause. Then the Doctor straightened up, grinned, and his tone lightened immediately. 'Well! There we are then! Thanks for that! Cheers, Big Fella!'

And he prodded the sword into the metallic ground, as if slightly embarrassed, and turned back to the others, leaving the Sycorax Leader standing behind him.

'Bravo!' shouted Harriet Jones, giving him a round of applause, as Rose rushed forwards, brimming with emotion.

'That says it all,' she said in a quieter tone. 'Bravo!'

'Yeah, not bad for a man in his jim-jams,' said the Doctor. Carefully, Rose helped him back into his dressing gown. It was quite the oddest thing; his proportions had changed. And yet somehow, when you were close to him, he felt exactly the same.

'Very Arthur Dent,' said the Doctor, looking down. 'Now there was a nice man,' which would have surprised Arthur tremendously if he'd heard it, seeing as every time they'd met, the Doctor had appeared almost outstandingly uninterested in killing Vogons, before beating him at Scrabble whilst simultaneously sharing long boring reminiscences with Ford about wild nights out they'd had together at college.

The Doctor stuck his new hand in his pocket to try it out. 'Hang on, what have we got here?' It emerged holding a satsuma, and Rose giggled as he furrowed his brow.

'Ah, that friend of your mother's, he does like his snacks, doesn't he? But doesn't that just sum up Christmas?' He tossed it in the air, and his new hand caught it perfectly. 'You go through all those presents, and right at the end, tucked away at the bottom, there's always one stupid old satsuma. I mean, who wants a satsuma? What are you ever going to do with a satsuma?'

Suddenly, behind him, the wounded Sycorax Leader got to his feet and seized the Doctor's broadsword, roaring and charging towards the Doctor, hell-bent on only one thing: his destruction.

The Doctor didn't even turn around.

As the Sycorax Leader raced towards him, he simply lobbed the satsuma at the wing switch on the side of the spaceship. Instantly, the flaps dislocated directly beneath the Sycorax Leader, and he vanished, simply dropped down into thin air; plummeting towards the Earth miles below with a dying scream.

The Doctor kept on walking. He still didn't turn around. His voice, when he spoke, was grim.

'No second chances,' he said coldly. 'I'm that sort of a man.'

19

Follow the Star

Harriet, Alex, Rose and Mickey followed the Doctor back into the amphitheatre, victorious. The army was cowed as they lined up in front of the TARDIS; the Doctor stood in the middle as he addressed the people of the Sycorax.

He spoke slowly and clearly, in no mood to be misunderstood.

'The Sycorax will leave,' he commanded, 'leave and never return. By the ancient rites of combat, I forbid you to scavenge here for the rest of Time. And when go you back to the stars and tell others of this planet… when you tell them of its riches, its people, its potential… When you talk of the Earth, then make sure that you tell them this.' His gaze swept the entire room and his voice grew louder still. 'It. Is. Defended.'

The engines whirred clunkily and a strange noise like gears grinding came out of nowhere, as the TARDIS rematerialised on an empty street.

'Where are we?' said Rose.

Mickey bundled out through the door. 'We're just off Bloxom Road—just round the corner from where we left. Look, no one up on the rooftops. Everything looks all right.' He was so happy he was practically jumping up and down. 'We did it!'

The Doctor held up a hand. 'Wait a minute… wait a minute…'

Above them the great Sycorax ship started to thrum; its engines shaking the ground. Very slowly, the great mass began to lift; accelerating away; leaving the Earth behind. A wind swept over them: backdraft. Papers and dust flew around, but nobody cared; they were all too busy celebrating.

'Go on, my son! Oh yeah!' shouted Mickey.

Rose jumped on his back cheerfully. 'Yeah! Don't come back!'

"IT. IS. DEFENDED!" quoted Mickey in a fair impression of the Doctor that made him frown. Rose jumped off him and threw her arms around a rather surprised Alex.

Meanwhile, the Doctor approached Harriet Jones.

'My Doctor,' she said proudly.

'Prime Minister,' he replied, and they hugged.

Harriet's mouth twitched. 'Absolutely the same man,' she said.

They turned to look up at the sky.

'Are there many more out there?' she asked.

'Oh, not just Sycorax,' the Doctor replied. 'Hundreds of species. Thousands of them. And the human race is drawing attention to itself. Every day you're sending out probes and messages and signals. This planet: it's so noisy. You're getting noticed... more and more.' He turned to look at her. 'You'd better get used to it.'

Harriet looked away.

'Rose?' Jackie came charging up the street, relief and crossness fighting for possession of her face. 'Rose! Oh, my God...'

'Mum!' cried Rose.

'Oh, talking of trouble,' the Doctor grinned, but Rose was already in her mother's arms.

'You did it, Rose!' Jackie murmured.

'He did it, Mum!' shouted Rose. 'He's the Doctor, and he did it... and you did it too!'

Jackie's eyebrows shot up. 'What?'

'It was the tea! Fixed his head.'

'That was all I needed: nice cup of tea,' said the Doctor supportively.

Jackie looked suddenly overwhelmed. 'I said so!' she exclaimed.

'And look at him!' said Rose.

She looked at her daughter's starstruck face, sensing trouble. 'Is it him, though? Is it really the Doctor?' Then she clocked Harriet Jones. 'Oh my God! It's the bleeding Prime Minister!'

The Doctor smiled. 'Come here you.' And in a way that, frankly, made Jackie doubt his Doctorish credentials more than anything he'd done yet—he hugged her.

Meanwhile, Alex beckoned Harriet Jones over to look at his phone. The telecoms satellites were back up, it seemed, after the sonic shockwave.

He glanced up at her. 'It's a message from Torchwood. They say they're ready.'

Harriet looked over at the five happy people. She didn't want to do this. But she was Prime Minister. She had a duty of care—a responsibility that went well beyond her own wishes. As the others chatted excitedly about pulling together a Christmas dinner, she took a deep breath.

'Tell them to fire,' she told Alex.

Alex looked at her for only a moment, then spoke softly into his phone. 'Fire at will.'

And she looked at the sky, and she looked at the group of happy people, and she stood her ground, and closed her eyes, and waited for what she knew must come.

Suddenly, a beam of light shot through the sky, emanating from somewhere in Docklands. It joined with another beam of light from a location south of the Thames.

The Doctor looked round, horrified.

Then another point of light joined it, and another, until Rose, and Mickey and Jackie and Alex were all twisting round to see where it was coming from.

All of them except Harriet, who knew so very, very well.

Above London the five points joined in the middle, forming a huge, intensely powerful pulse, which punched up through the atmosphere and burst into space, where the Sycorax ship was already gliding away into the void.

It slammed into the ship, which burst apart.

From the Earth they could see it: parts of the disintegrating vessel, like a shower of meteors in the sky. Jackie had a hand over her mouth.

'What is that?' Rose was crying. 'What is it?'

Harriet glanced at Rose who was staring at her in disbelief. Then she gathered her courage and looked at the Doctor.

'I really am so sorry,' she said truthfully.

He looked right at her, and the disappointment in his gaze was worse than the anger.

'That was murder,' he said baldly.

Harriet squared up.

'That was defence. Defence that's been adapted from alien technology. A ship that fell to Earth ten years ago.'

'But they were *leaving*.'

'You saw the way their leader broke his word to you moments after he'd sworn it. You said yourself, Doctor:

they'd go back to the stars and tell others about the Earth.' Harriet gazed up at him with a sudden anger. 'I'm sorry, Doctor, but you're not here all the time. You come and go, and sometimes people die. It happened today: Mr Llewellyn and the Major, they were murdered. They died right in front of me while you lay sleeping. And if you're not here, we have to defend ourselves.'

The Doctor stared at her. 'Britain's Golden Age,' he said, his tone dripping with contempt.

'It comes with a price,' she shot back.

They stared at one another for a long moment. Then the Doctor shook his head.

'I gave them the the wrong warning,' he said. 'I should've told them to run, as fast as they can... to run and hide because the monsters are coming: the human race!'

'Those are the people I represent!' Quivering in self-righteous anger, Harriet Jones pointed at the Doctor's friends. 'I acted on their behalf.'

'Then I should've stopped you,' said the Doctor

'Then what does that make you, Doctor?' she demanded. 'Another alien threat?'

The Doctor took a step forward at that. 'Don't challenge me, Harriet Jones. 'Cos I'm a completely new man. And I don't need swordfights to beat you. I'm stronger than that. I could bring down your government with a single word.'

Harriet remained unbowed. 'You're the most remarkable man I've ever met, but I don't think you're quite capable of that.'

'No, you're right,' said the Doctor. 'Not a single word...' He counted out on his fingers. 'Just six.'

'I don't think so.'

'Six words.'

'Stop it!'

'Six,' the Doctor repeated, walking around her, not taking his eyes from her.

She held his gaze, trying not to show her fear. She felt a sudden urge to cough. But she would not yield. They both held each other's gaze, and neither would back down.

Then, still keeping his eyes fixed on Harriet, the Doctor moved, slowly and carefully, towards Alex.

And Harriet felt scared; scared, because this ruthlessness in him: *this* really was new.

Without taking his eyes from the Prime Minister, the Doctor motioned for Alex to take off his earpiece. Then he simply whispered, straight into his ear: 'Don't you think she looks tired?'

And he walked straight off, briskly, calling out to the others, 'Come on! We're going!'

The Doctor, Mickey, Rose and Jackie walked off down the street, leaving Harriet Jones behind them.

She rushed up to Alex. 'What did he say? Well? What did he tell you?'

Awkwardly, Alex shrugged. 'It… was nothing, really.'

'What did he say?'

'Nothing! I don't know!'

Harriet turned from him, harried and alarmed. 'Doctor!' she shouted after him. 'What did you say?'

The Doctor ignored her, and the others followed suit, leaving her alone, leaving her desperately calling after him; shouting over and over the words that could change nothing now: 'I'm sorry. *I'm sorry!*'

20

All I Want for Christmas Is You

The wardrobe in the TARDIS is vast. Self-cleaning, entirely crammed with every conceivable type of outfit for most occasions, from Vyxar System state balls, which lasted anything up to four lunar rotations, to anything that might help you out at a Romansch evensong.

The Doctor picked up a soldier's uniform. Absolutely not. He looked around, unsure. He needed something to blend in… something he could run in, if running was required, and in his lengthy experience, running was often required. Something that would suit him. Or did he care about that? He wasn't sure. He grabbed a red hussar jacket. No. But no more black. What colour was his hair again? Brown, Rose had said. Not ginger, but … OK. Brown then. He glanced up and down—and then he saw a slim-cut brown pinstriped suit and snatched it from the rack. He'd never been able to get into it before. But maybe now…

He tried it on. Oh yes. He—quite wrongly—did not consider himself to be a vain man, but turning around in front of the mirror, he couldn't help but admire the effect. Yes. This would definitely do. He ran his tongue over his strange new teeth one last time. Then he squinted. His reflection looked a little fuzzy. That was odd. But he was going to be late for dinner.

Mickey was carving the turkey—very badly—and Rose was serving the sprouts as the Doctor walked quietly into the house.

The delighted look on Rose's face told him all he needed to know. The relief this brought was like warm water sluicing through him. The Sycorax hadn't worried him much—not for a second. However, the possibility that Rose of all people—that Rose, his heart of the TARDIS, might not recognise him, nor accept him… He would never have admitted to himself how close to an unbearable thought that was.

They sat down at the table and he pulled a cracker with her. She screamed, absurdly. He won, but handed her the bigger half anyway, because he liked to see her smile, and she did. She pulled out the party hat.

'It's pink! Mum, it should be yours!'

Jackie smiled as Rose put the hat on anyway, laughing. It wasn't pink, thought the Doctor. It was rose. Then he stopped himself. He felt mushy. He didn't want to be mushy. What was he even doing, sitting down for Christmas lunch? This wasn't him. This wasn't his family. And he didn't play happy families. Not any more.

Mickey was watching them both, his festive mood vanishing in an instant. The Doctor, sat there wearing his new body, looked like he'd had his feet under the table here for years. The way Rose was laughing...

On his part, the Doctor watched Rose laugh and felt a faint stab of alarm; a slight realisation that he was out of his depth in some tantalising, difficult fashion he could only sense and not truly understand. Rose was talking, but he couldn't hear her. Then he noticed she was pointing at the TV.

'Look! It's Harriet Jones!'

They all turned to look, and the Doctor realised the screen was fuzzy too. Aha. He supposed this was payback for the slim-cut suit and luxuriant hair; and he pulled a pair of black-rimmed spectacles from his pocket, left for just such an occasion, and put them on.

A journalist was speaking.

'Prime Minister, is it true you are no longer fit to be in power?'

Underneath the interview, the caption ran: Alien Invasion. But just behind that scrolled: PM Healthcare—Unfit for Duty?

'No,' said Harriet Jones, turning away to cough crossly. 'Now, can we talk about other things?'

The Doctor watched, his gaze steely.

'*I repeat the question: Is it true that you're unfit for office?*'

'Look' said Harriet, entirely in a flap. 'There is nothing wrong with my health! I don't know where these stories are coming from! And a vote of no confidence is completely unjustified!'

The phone rang and Jackie left to answer it.

'*Are you going to resign?*' badgered the journalist.

'On today of all days?' Harriet seemed utterly frustrated. 'I'm fine. Look at me. I'm fine. I look fine. I feel fine.'

Jackie came back into the room.

'It's Beth,' said Jackie. 'She says go and look outside.'

The Doctor took off his glasses. He'd seen more than enough on the television screen.

'Why?' said Rose.

'I dunno, just go outside and look! Come on, shift!'

Outside, even though many windows were boarded up, there were people everywhere, laughing and throwing snowballs around as light flakes fell on them.

'Oh that's beautiful!' said Rose. 'What are they, meteors?'

The Doctor's eyes were full of sadness. 'It's the spaceship,' he said quietly. 'Breaking up in the atmosphere. This isn't snow. It's ash.'

'OK,' said Rose. 'Not so beautiful.'

The Doctor looked around. 'And this is the brand new planet Earth. No denying the existence of aliens now. Everyone saw it…'

Rose had a lump in her throat. Everything was new. Completely changed. And she'd been wanting to wait until after dinner, after they'd enjoyed just a bit of Christmas; after she'd had a chance to talk to her mother.

But she couldn't wait. She couldn't. She had to know.

'Doctor…' Rose stared at the grey ash on the ground so she didn't have to watch his face, in case it shifted; in case he looked sorry and regretful as he told her something she didn't want to hear. 'What about you?' she ventured, gently. 'What are you going to do next?'

The Doctor stiffened. That wasn't a 'we'. That wasn't a 'What are *we* going to do next?' Was she trying to let him down gently? Was dinner a farewell? If he'd known, he'd have skipped the sprouts. He sighed. What else could he say?

'Well… back to the TARDIS. Same old life.'

His face had changed. His world did not; he couldn't blame Rose for not wanting to continue. She must have really… she must have been very fond of the last incarnation. Some change was too much.

She looked up at him, tentative and nervous.

'On… on your own?'

He answered too quickly he realised, even as he was speaking.

'Why, don't you want to come?'

There was a long pause as each tried to gauge the other's mood. Rose could feel her heart speed up. Would he? Could she?

'Well, yeah,' she said, stiffening, preparing for rejection.

'Do you, though?' said the Doctor, wary she was just being polite.

'Yeah!' said Rose again, more emphatically this time.

'I just thought…'cos I changed…'

'Yeah, I thought…. 'cos you changed… you might not want me any more.'

A huge beaming smile cracked across the Doctor's face. 'Oh, I'd *love* you to come!'

Rose mirrored his expression, filled with glee. 'Okay!' she said, and they beamed at each other like idiots, as if they were the only people there—although they were not.

Mickey stared at the ground. Watching another man make Rose happy was too much for him to bear. 'You're never going to stay, are you?'

Rose looked at him, not understanding; not wanting to understand. She never did.

'There's just so much out there,' she said. 'So much to see… I've got to.'

'Yeah,' said Mickey.

Jackie heaved a sigh. 'Well, I reckon you're mad, the pair of you. It's like you go looking for trouble.'

'Trouble's just the bits in between!' said the Doctor joyfully. He pointed her face up to the stars. 'It's all waiting out there, Jackie. Everything's brand new to me...'

Rose smiled happily watching him. She couldn't take her eyes off him, thought Mickey crossly. Not for a minute. And the other guy. That guy had been old, and a bit weird looking. This one... this one was young. And handsome. And she stared at him like he was chocolate cake.

The Doctor was still talking.

'All those planets... creatures and horizons... I haven't seen them yet! Not with these eyes... and it is gonna be... fantastic!'

Rose grinned; he sounded so like himself. Then she looked down. His hand was held out towards her; just as it had always been; just as she'd dreaded it might never be again. Then she remembered it was his new hand.

'That hand of yours still gives me the creeps,' she said, but the Doctor merely grinned, and waggled his fingers at her, and she took it, of course, as she had known she would, because it was the only place her hand ever wanted to be. She moved closer as they looked up at the sky. A flare came down, then another, brighter cascade of sparks in the sky.

'I miss him,' she said, quietly.

'So do I,' said the Doctor.

They smiled, a little sadly, at one another. Then Rose perked up again.

'So, where're we going go first?' she asked him.

'Um… that way.' The Doctor pointed at a tiny spot in the night sky. 'No, hold on… that way,' he said, moving his finger incrementally.

Rose pointed too. 'That way?'

The Doctor looked at her. 'Do you think?'

She nodded, softly. 'Yeah,' she said. 'That way.'

And, oblivious to anyone else, they stared at one another, then up at the light of the stars.

Epilogue

Jackie went home, and turned up the telly as loud as it would go, and called Bev, and put the kettle on and pottered about, making noise, clearing up, doing anything she could to distract herself, so she didn't have to hear that noise.

That damned noise.

Sometimes, the only noise she longed for. Other times, like now, the noise she dreaded most. The grinding of the gears...

And Mickey didn't go home, but walked the cold streets all night, watching the festive revellers, alone, powering on, trying to make his brain tired enough to sleep; trying to wear himself out enough so he could stop feeling so much, all the time. Stop missing her, every second of every day.

And five miles north, in the Tower of London, Sally Jacobs was back at her desk; sitting with the same mug she'd used that morning; trying to take in the terrible reality of what had happened. Four people had been teleported from the office. Two had returned, and as the others vocally mourned their decent boss, she mourned them both.

But there was work to do; more than ever. For the eye of the universe had opened and blinked slowly in their direction. They had all seen it. They had all felt it.

And as the old year turned and a new year began, the Earth would hold its breath.

Author's Afterword

A Target book! I have said it before, and it's true: if you want to become a lifelong *Doctor Who* fan, being born in the very early 1970s is a very good place to start, because it made you more or less seven years old by the time *Horror of Fang Rock* and *City of Death* and all that awesome stuff came out. But of course in those days, you only got to see them once (plus the BBC two early evening repeats).

So I grew up on the Target novelisations: a little line of distinctively scented, plastic-lined paperbacks in Prestwick library.

Terrance Dicks was my favourite of course, but Ian Marter would do. In fact, I think with the limitless Imagination Budget books have, I actually preferred them to when years later, I finally caught up with the DVDs. My only problem was how quickly you could read them: you could only borrow four books a week from my local library, and there was absolutely no way you could make four Targets stretch that long.

But oh the joy of finding a new one on the shelves. My absolute favourite was *The Deadly Assassin*, and I must have read and returned it eight times. I never owned one—buying books was for rich people—which is why when people talk about closing down libraries I get a bit foam-y at the mouth.

Ridiculously, back in 2005, I was unsure about David Tennant becoming the new Doctor. I hadn't seen *Casanova*, although I remembered his wonderful performance as the beautiful damaged child in the exceptional *Taking Over the Asylum*.

But in my opinion nobody could touch what Christopher Eccleston had done: taken what was at the time a massive risk and turned it into the biggest hit the BBC had had for years. Chris wasn't wacky; he was earthy, sincere, mindbogglingly sexy, a proper grown-up, and you believed every single thing he said. So casting a skinny, pretty boy seemed a strange step to take, and covering up his Scottish accent simply bizarre.

Fortunately I was totally and utterly wrong, although you have to watch quite a lot of him being unconscious before you get to this: a truly fantastic tease by the production team, who knew exactly what treasure they had on their hands. *The Christmas Invasion* is an episode so inventive and funny and terrific that it started the tradition of yuletide episodes that continues to this day (with, it has to be said, occasionally mixed results).

The episode, with its clever, sinister blood control, ugly chatty monsters and terrific climactic battle, feels like an air punch, a wonderful, bravura introduction that immediately makes you realise you're in safe hands (three of which belong to the new Doctor).

'Don't you think she looks tired?' has entered the lexicon of people who haven't even seen the show. (In a particularly 2017 move, by the way, my Harriet also has a cough.) It also has my absolute favourite type of set-up: utter normality twisted on its head.

What's more normal than eating satsumas at Christmas? Peril showing up in your own living room is always more frightening to me than an alien landscape (which is why I think the scariest nu-*Who* episode by far is *Turn Left*), even if it comes in the guise of a rotating bandsaw Christmas tree.

Within the year, David would take the show from a hit to a phenomenon. Friends of mine (particularly, I noticed, mums) who had never before taken an interest in my peculiar side career suddenly wanted to discuss the finer points of *Silence in the Library* and *Blink*. The fake regeneration in *The Stolen Earth* became a national crisis. And the very clear and certain, undeniable inevitability that this Doctor and Rose would fall madly in love is on the page from the very start.

I have so enjoyed reliving this episode here. Although the stories that mark *Doctor Who* moving into its Second Imperial Phase don't really date, I did enjoy Mickey still having to ask to plug his modem into the phone line. (What a brilliant hacker he was too, on dial-up. Wasted working in that garage, if you ask me.)

You can tell Russell T Davies isn't a novelist, by the way, because a novelist would never, ever call a character Llewellyn; it is an absolute toad of a word to type. Try it and you'll see what I mean. Fortunately, what Russell is, is a genius, which made the rest of my job not just easy but an utter joy. I am still slightly overwhelmed that the first Target book I will ever own will be one that I have written—and I so hope you've enjoyed it.

Best wishes,

Jenny
December 2017

With grateful thanks to Norah Perkins, Curtis Brown and the Douglas Adams Estate.

Also: Russell T Davies particularly for his patience with my stupid questions and for being SO FUNNY; Steve Cole, Albert DePetrillo and all at BBC Books; James Goss; Richard Osman (he knows why); Matthew Nicolson and family, and Jo Unwin.